The Mysterious Case of the Missing Ghost

A Redemption Detective Agency Mystery

Books and series by Michele Pariza Wacek

Redemption Detective Agency
(Cozy Mysteries)
A spin-off from the Charlie Kingsley series.
https://MPWNovels.com/r/da_ghost

Charlie Kingsley Mysteries
(Cozy Mysteries)
See all of Charlie's adventures here.
https://MPWnovels.com/r/ck_ghost

Secrets of Redemption series
(Pychological Thrillers)
The flagship series that started it all.
https://MPWnovels.com/r/rd_ghost

Mysteries of Redemption
(Psychological Thrillers)
A spin-off from the Secrets of Redemption series.
https://MPWnovels.com/r/mr_ghost

Riverview Mysteries
(standalone Pychological Thrillers)
These stories take place in Riverview, which is near Redemption.
https://MPWnovels.com/r/rm_ghost

The Mysterious Case of the Missing Ghost

A Redemption Detective Agency Mystery

by Michele Pariza Wacek

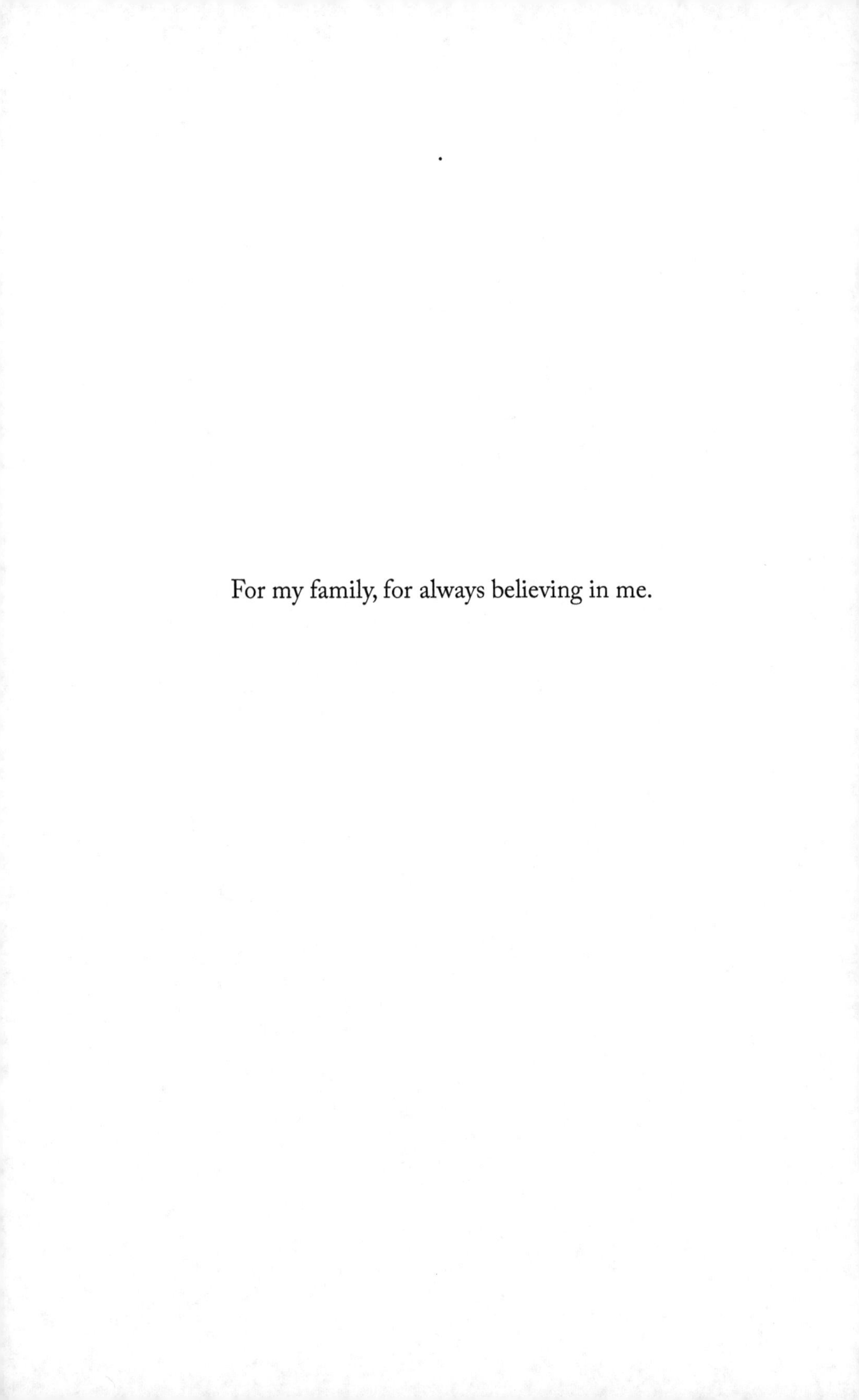

For my family, for always believing in me.

Chapter 1

"My husband is missing. Can you find him?"

I straightened up, pressing the phone tighter against my ear. The voice was frail and thin, and I wondered if I had heard her correctly. "Did you say your husband is *missing?*"

"Yes. I need help finding him. Can you do that?"

"Is this an emergency? Have you tried calling the police?"

"Oh, the police," the voice scoffed. "They can't do anything."

That probably meant it wasn't an emergency, which also indicated her husband had either left on his own accord, or something else had happened to him—something unrelated to foul play. It wasn't against the law for an adult to disappear, so unless there was evidence that he had been taken against his will, the police likely wouldn't get involved. I suspected most of the time, in most other places, there wasn't much in the way of a "something else" option ... but this was Redemption, Wisconsin, after all. Here, disappearances were far higher than the national average.

I reached for a pen and yellow pad of paper. "When was the last time you saw him?"

There was a pause. "Well, it's been years since I've seen him."

My pen hovered over the pad. "Years?"

"Oooh, I think Emily has a new client on the phone," Aunt Tilde said, elbowing Mildred. They had been fiddling with the coffee maker all morning, but I was unclear as to whether there was actually a problem with the equipment, or if they were just too busy talking to make any coffee. I waved at her to be quiet.

"Well, my eyes, you know. They're not what they used to be." She sounded apologetic, and I immediately felt bad. This poor woman probably had cataracts, or had maybe even gone blind, and my first thought was that her husband had been missing for a decade, and she was only now getting around to calling someone about it. "But I know he was here two days ago."

"So he's been missing for two days?"

"I think so." There was a hitch in her voice. "I'm worried about him."

"Of course you are, Mrs. …"

"It's Jonasburg, but you can call me Ruth."

I wrote her name down on the yellow pad. "Ruth, then. Can you tell me a little bit about the circumstances surrounding his disappearance? Maybe start with before he left …"

I could hear her swallow. "That's just it. We had a … well, maybe not a *fight*, but definitely a disagreement, and … oh … I don't know what I'll do, if that really was my last interaction with him."

"Let's not think about that now," I said quickly. "Why don't we set up a time to discuss your situation in more detail? Would you be able to come to the office?"

"Oh dear, I'm really not good with driving anymore. Do you think you could come to the house?"

"Sure," I said, quickly jotting down her address as she rattled it off. We agreed to meet later that afternoon, and I hung up the phone.

Both Mildred and Aunt Tilde were watching me closely. "So, tell us about our new client," Aunt Tilde said excitedly.

A nurse who got bored during her retirement and decided it would be fun to open a detective agency with absolutely zero training or experience, Aunt Tilde definitely danced to the beat of her own drum. Today, she was dressed in bright pinks and purples, which didn't clash as much as you might think with her bright-orange hair and matching glasses.

"It's about time we got one," Mildred chimed in, giving me a stern look over her glasses, as though our lack of clients was somehow my fault. Mildred was a retired teacher who had jumped at the chance to join her old friend in her newest venture. She dressed far more conservatively than my aunt, though, in pressed pantsuits. She also had her hair done twice a week and wore a little too much perfume. Today, she was dressed in a pale-green pantsuit accented by a single strand of pearls.

"She's not an official client yet," I said. "She wants to see if we can help her find her husband."

Mildred perked up. "Another cheating husband case. Hopefully, we can redeem ourselves with this one."

"Her husband is missing," I said. "That doesn't mean he's cheating."

Mildred waved her hand. "Of course it does. What other explanation would there be?"

"We shouldn't assume he's cheating," Aunt Tilde said. "That's why we investigate."

Mildred raised a nicely shaped eyebrow. "Okay, why do *you* think he's missing, then?"

Aunt Tilde shrugged. "Maybe he got lost."

"What, like he went to the store for cigarettes and never came home?"

"It's possible," Aunt Tilde insisted before letting out a sigh and relenting. "Okay, you're probably right. He's cheating on her."

"Maybe we should hear the entire story before we make assumptions," I suggested.

"I agree. We should get all the details, so we can catch him in the act," Mildred said before flattening her lips, which were covered in bright-pink lipstick, in disapproval. "We don't want to screw it up this time."

"I don't think this case is going to be like Jan's," I said.

"How do you know?" Mildred asked.

"Well, for one, we're looking for a missing husband, not for proof that her husband is cheating on her," I said.

Mildred waved her hand again. "I told you … same thing."

Great. At this rate, I was going to have to find some excuse to keep Mildred from attending the initial meeting. I could already picture her browbeating poor Ruth and insisting her husband had run off with the grocery clerk.

"When is the meeting?" Aunt Tilde asked, as if reading my mind.

Ugh. "This afternoon." I gave Mildred a hard look. "If you come, you can't tell her that her husband is cheating on her. She's very upset. They had a fight before he disappeared."

Mildred looked miffed. "Emily, of course I wouldn't say it. You know me better than that."

Yes, yes, I do know you, and that's why I'm telling you not to. I bit down on my tongue to keep the words from coming out and forced a smile instead. "I just wanted you to know what I know before the meeting. That way, we're all on the same page."

"Good, we should be," Mildred said briskly. "When the time is right, we can tell her the truth about her husband. Not a minute before."

I sighed.

***

"Here we are," I said, gesturing toward a dark-brown two-story house with white trim. Aunt Tilde was driving her signature pink Cadillac with Mildred next to her and me in the backseat.

Aunt Tilde's brows knit together as she leaned over to look through the passenger window. "Isn't this Ruth's house?"

"Yeah, you know her?"

Aunt Tilde twisted her head around to look at me. "Ruth's husband is missing?"

"Yeah." I suddenly felt a chill. "Why? What's wrong? Is her husband sick or something?"

"You could say that," Mildred said.

"What does that mean?" I asked.

Aunt Tilde parked the car by the curb and shot Mildred an unreadable look. "It means it's time to meet our new client." She unbuckled her seatbelt, got out of the car, and started walking determinedly up the driveway. Much to my surprise, Mildred meekly followed without saying a word. I was so taken aback, I sat there for a moment before realizing that at the rate they were going, they would likely start the meeting without me, so I hurriedly got out as well and trotted toward them to catch up.

Aunt Tilde reached the door first, but before she could ring the bell, Ruth opened the door. "Oh Tilde, I'm so glad you're here," she said, her face a wreath of smiles. She looked older than Aunt Tilde, and Mildred for that matter, but I knew that didn't mean she actually was. Her clothes were clean and pressed but faded—a pink and yellow flowered blouse with pink pants—and her gray hair was like dandelion puffs around her head. She wore no makeup, other than bright-pink lipstick, and thick, black-framed glasses.

Aunt Tilde leaned in to give her a half-hug. "Ruth, it's so nice to see you! I'm sorry I haven't been by to visit recently."

"Oh, nonsense," Ruth said, giving Tilde's arm a gentle swat. "Heavens, you've been busy! You've started a detective agency!"

"Well, yes, but I couldn't have done it without my niece, Emily," Aunt Tilde said, gesturing toward me.

"Of course," Ruth said, her sharp eyes giving me a once-over. Something niggled at the back of my head about that, but I couldn't quite put my finger on it. "It's lovely to meet you," Ruth continued, reaching for my hand. She squeezed it, and I could feel her paper-dry skin. "It's wonderful when you can work with your family, isn't it?"

"It's been one of the best parts of opening the agency," Aunt Tilde said, giving me a warm smile that I felt deep in my chest.

Ruth let go of my hand and turned to Mildred. "And Mildred, it's so wonderful to see you, as well. Are you part of the agency too?"

"You better believe it," Mildred said. "I'm the best detective they have."

I tried not to roll my eyes.

"Come in, come in," Ruth said, stepping back from the door so we could enter. The entryway opened onto a large living room to the right with a set of stairs to the left. Further down the hallway, I could see what appeared to be a kitchen. The house was tidy, but not overly so. There was a stack of mail on the coffee table in the living room and a thin layer of dust on the mirror in the hallway. The house smelled of coffee, cinnamon, and an overly aggressive floral air freshener. It was also warm and humid, like she hadn't used an air conditioner in a while. Not that I completely minded; most of the time, people cranked the air conditioning up too high for my liking, but this house felt pretty stuffy. "Would you like something to drink?"

"Oh, we don't want to cause you any trouble," Aunt Tilde said.

Ruth waved her hand. "No trouble. I have a pot of coffee I just finished brewing. I'll bring you all a cup, if you want to have a seat in the living room."

"Coffee sounds lovely, thank you," Aunt Tilde said as we made our way toward the stiff couch, loveseat, and chair ensemble in beige and blue plaid. I sat down on the chair, pulling out my notebook and pen, while Aunt Tilde and Mildred took the couch. Ruth followed a few minutes later, carrying a tray with the coffeepot, four mugs, cream, sugar, and a plate of what looked like homemade cookies. She pushed the pile of mail aside and a couple of envelopes tipped onto the floor. Aunt Tilde scooped them up as Ruth passed coffee in delicate white and gold china cups with matching saucers. I smiled as I accepted mine, even though it meant balancing my coffee on one knee and my notebook on the other.

"So, tell us about Hank," Aunt Tilde said as she doctored her coffee with cream and sugar.

Ruth's hand trembled, causing her cup to clink against her saucer, and she put it down. "It's dreadful. I'm so worried. I think he's really gone."

Aunt Tilde leaned over to put a hand on Ruth's knee. "Of course Hank isn't gone. He loved you too much. He'll always be here."

"I'm sure he's still watching over you," Mildred said, although it sounded like she was choking on the words.

Loved? As in past tense? Watching over you? This didn't sound like a missing husband. It sounded like a deceased husband. But if he was deceased, why did she say he was missing? Did she have dementia? Is that why Mildred looked so miserable? But if she had dementia, how could she be living alone in such a big house?

I studied Ruth, watching her as she dabbed delicately at her eyes, trying to see if there were any signs of dementia, and just like that, the thing that had been niggling at me since we stepped into Ruth's house suddenly popped into my brain.

Ruth wasn't blind. Yes, her glasses looked pretty thick, but she had no trouble pouring coffee into tiny, delicate china cups and passing them around. So, if she hadn't physically seen her husband in years, that probably meant her husband had been dead for years, and if that were the case, then what were we doing here?

"I'm sorry," I broke in, and all three women swung their heads around to look at me. "But is your husband … did he pass away?"

"Yes, it's been ten years now," Ruth said.

I blinked. Ten *years?* "Oh … um … I'm so sorry to hear that. Did you … remarry?"

"Oh no." Ruth pressed her hand to her heart. "Hank was my one and only. No one could ever replace him."

"He was one-of-a-kind," Aunt Tilde agreed. Next to her, Mildred nodded.

I stared at the three women as I replayed my conversation with Ruth back in my head. No, I was sure she said her husband was missing. But how could he be missing? Unless … I swallowed hard. *Oh no. Please don't say his ashes. Or, even worse, his body.*

"I'm so sorry, but I'm a little confused," I said. "I thought we were here because you said your husband is missing."

Ruth bobbed her head up and down. "Indeed. He is missing. He disappeared two days ago, and I haven't seen him-well … *heard* from him, since."

I eyed Aunt Tilde and Mildred, but neither of them looked like this was surprising news to them. Nor did they look particularly alarmed that it appeared their friend was operating under a severe delusion.

Apparently, it was all up to me. "I'm sorry, but exactly what disappeared? Your husband's … ashes?" At the last minute, I found myself unable to say the word "body." Or "corpse."

Ruth burst out laughing. Aunt Tilde joined her, but Mildred was surprisingly silent. "Oh no," Ruth said, when she could finally talk. "Of course not. You poor thing. You thought I was talking to my husband's dead body. No wonder you look so confused."

Relieved, I started smiling as well, even while acknowledging Mildred's lack thereof. It must be something harmless, I decided. Maybe she had a pet with the name "Husband," although the idea of embarking on another missing-dog case gave me the chills. "So who were you talking about?"

"His ghost, dear," Ruth said. "What else would I be talking about?"

Chapter 2

My smile vanished. "Ghost? You mean your husband's ghost?"

"Of course!" Ruth gave me a warm smile as she sipped her coffee. Mildred rolled her eyes.

"I'm sorry, but I'm not sure I understand. Your husband's ghost …"

"Lives here with me, yes," Ruth said before her eyes started welling up with tears. "At least he did. Now I don't know where he is."

"Maybe you should start at the beginning," Aunt Tilde suggested gently.

Ruth nodded and dabbed at her eyes. "Ten years ago, my husband died. It was very unexpected."

"I'm so sorry," I said. "So he wasn't sick or anything?" I was assuming he died at home, seeing as she was claiming to have been conversing with his ghost.

She shook her head. "He had an accident coming home from work. It was just … it was awful. He never even made it to the hospital."

"Truly dreadful," Aunt Tilde chimed in.

"Oh geez. That's horrible," I said.

Ruth's hands started shaking again, and she moved to put her cup down onto the table. "Those first few weeks were truly the worst time of my life. I felt so alone. As much as we had wanted children, unfortunately, that never happened. And we had just put down our beloved cat Stormy a couple of weeks before and hadn't gotten around to getting another cat. So it was just … us. And then, it was just me."

My heart broke for her, but I didn't know what to say. I felt foolish telling her how sorry I was, even though I was. Instead, I kept my mouth shut and let her collect herself.

She finally did, sitting back in her chair and giving me a warm smile. "So you can imagine how happy I was when I discovered that Hank's ghost had come back for me."

I forced myself to keep my expression neutral. "Yes, I can imagine that must have been a huge comfort. But how did you know it was Hank's ghost?" *Versus another ghost,* I thought but didn't say out loud.

Her smile turned secretive. "A wife always knows."

I couldn't help myself; my eyebrows went up.

She giggled. "Not like that. I just mean … well, for starters, I could smell him."

"You could smell … a ghost?"

She nodded. "That's how I first knew he was with me. It was his smell. It was just so strong, like he was in the room with me. Of course, at first, I just dismissed it. I thought I was just imagining things, or maybe his scent was lingering on his clothes. I hadn't done any laundry in weeks—not even my own clothes, never mind his. Nor the sheets or the towels. I wanted to try to keep his scent around as long as possible, but despite everything I had been doing, it was starting to fade. And I was upset. It felt like I was losing him all over again.

"But then, that afternoon, I could *smell* him. Really smell him. Even though I felt a little silly, I said, out loud, 'Hank, is that you?' And he answered."

I had been lifting my coffee cup to take a sip, and I nearly dropped it. "He *answered?*"

She nodded eagerly. "He did. It was amazing and shocking at the same time. My heart nearly stopped in my chest. I had to sit down."

"What did he … what did he say?"

She shook her head. "It wasn't like that. He didn't speak, at least not while I was awake. Sometimes, in my dreams, we would talk and talk … it was just like old times, really. Oh, how I missed those times." She pressed a hand against her chest again.

"So why didn't he talk when you were awake?"

She gave me a look, as if it should have been obvious. "It's not like ghosts have vocal cords. They're not like us. They can't talk."

"Emily is new to Redemption," Aunt Tilde said, almost as an aside. "She hasn't met any ghosts yet."

Ruth's face softened. "Oh, of course. I should have realized that."

Redemption, Wisconsin, had a long history of strange and unusual events, including far more disappearances than a town its size should have. It can all be traced back to 1888, when all the adults disappeared, leaving only the children. To this day, no one knows what happened to the adults. The children all swore up and down they had no idea what had happened. They woke up, and the adults were gone. Ever since, Redemption had been a hotbed for mysterious and unexplained happenings, including its share of ghosts and hauntings.

That said, I didn't think that meant that every resident had first-hand experience with a ghost. It was on the tip of my tongue to ask if ghost anatomy was common knowledge in Redemption, but then I realized I didn't actually want to know the answer. One of the few lessons my mother instilled in me that I still followed was to not ask questions I didn't want answers to.

"Anyway, Hank communicated the way I imagine most ghosts do," Ruth continued, as though living with a ghost was a perfectly normal occurrence. "Flickering the lights, knocking things over, hiding things. Oh, he could be mischievous, my Hank. He especially loved hiding my keys on me."

I wondered how ghosts could move keys without hands, since apparently, they weren't able to talk without vocal cords, but again, I decided that was another question I didn't want the answer to. "So how did Hank answer that first time?"

"Flickering the lights," Ruth said immediately. "That was his go-to. One flicker for yes, two for no. It took a bit to get used to having conversations in which he could only give me yes or no answers, but we managed. Occasionally, he would also leave a message for me on the fridge."

"The ... fridge?" I asked, my voice faint, trying to picture what he could possibly have been doing. Was he arranging the leftovers so they resembled some sort of code that only she could crack? Perhaps the macaroni and cheese meant he thought something was cheesy, or maybe bland and boring. Or perhaps he was actually writing words and using condiments as ink. I could imagine the fridge covered with a ketchup confession: "Ruth, I'm so sorry I did this to you."

She nodded eagerly, picking up her coffee cup and taking a sip. "I have some magnetic letters and a little board I bought shortly after I knew he was back. He didn't use them a lot. I think they were a little exhausting for him, not that he would ever admit that. You know how men are." She rolled her eyes. "But when he had something important to tell me, they were a huge blessing."

"I can imagine," I said, and swallowed. "So how long was Hank here? As a ghost, I mean."

She spread her hands out. "He's been here the whole time, until …" she paused, her eyes misting again. "Until two days ago."

"When Hank … the ghost … went missing," I said.

She nodded. Her hands began trembling again, so she placed her cup back down on the table. "I just feel like I've lost him all over again."

"Oh honey, that's not true," Aunt Tilde said, reaching out to squeeze her hand. "He'll turn up again. You'll see."

"Yeah, he probably just had to attend a ghost convention or something. I'm sure he'll be home soon," Mildred said drily. Aunt Tilde glared at her, and Mildred mouthed, "What?" in response. Aunt Tilde shook her head in disgust and went back to rubbing Ruth's hand, who luckily, was too upset to notice the exchange.

"I don't know, Tilde," Ruth said, her chest heaving. "He's never done anything like this before. I'm really worried about him."

"What exactly did he do?" Aunt Tilde asked.

It took her a moment before she got herself under control enough to answer. "We had a … disagreement."

"A disagreement?" Mildred asked. Aunt Tilde shot her another look, and Mildred closed her mouth.

"It was silly, really," Ruth said, shaking her head. "You'd think after all this time, Hank would know how to replace the toilet paper correctly."

I blinked, sure I hadn't heard correctly. "Um, Hank replaces the toilet paper?"

She looked at me in surprise. "Of course he does, if he's the one who uses the last of the roll."

Ghosts didn't have vocal cords, but somehow still had a need for toilet paper? "Hank would still use … the toilet?"

"No, no, no. Of course not," Ruth said. "But sometimes, he needed the toilet paper for other things."

"Other … things?" I couldn't even begin to imagine what a ghost might need toilet paper for.

She fluttered her hands. "You know. Killing a bug or wiping up a spill. Occasionally, he would decorate the bathroom with it." She rolled her eyes fondly. "Hank was such a prankster. And every now and then, he would use it to leave me messages."

"I thought that's what the refrigerator magnets were for."

She reached down to pick up her coffee cup as she continued flapping one of her hands. "The problem with the refrigerator magnets is that I only had one of each letter of the alphabet, so depending on what he wanted to tell me, he might not have enough letters."

"I think Nora wrote her entire business plan for her used bookstore on a couple of squares of toilet paper," Aunt Tilde mused.

"Why doesn't that surprise me?" Mildred muttered. Aunt Tilde frowned at her, and Mildred shut her mouth. I tried to suppress a smile. Mildred and I didn't always see eye to eye, but in this situation, I completely agreed with her.

Nora was the fourth member of The Redemption Detective Agency. She owned a used bookstore that was located in the same strip mall as the agency and would often pop in to see if there were any cases she could help solve. If there weren't any, she would bring mystery books for us to read.

"Anyway, the long-standing rule in our house is that whoever uses up the toilet paper needs to put a new roll in the holder," Ruth said. "This has always been the case, since the day we were married. So how can he still do it wrong after all these years?"

"That's a good question," Mildred said.

I was still stuck on the image of a ghost not just replacing a roll of toilet paper, but doing it wrong, to boot. "So I'm guessing the toilet paper was 'under' … so it was hanging down in the back?"

Ruth stared at me as if I had grown another head. "No, that's the right way," Ruth said. "You always want the toilet paper under."

"I always thought over was better," Mildred said. "It's easier to keep clean."

Ruth shook her head. "Under is better. It's easier to use."

"Under also makes it easier to decorate your bathroom with toilet paper," I said, demonstrating with my hands. "Maybe that's what was going on with your bathroom."

"Oh, that doesn't matter. Hank would find a way," Ruth said. "Or Sally."

"Wait, Sally? Who's Sally?" *Oh, please don't say another ghost.*

"The cat," Ruth said. Thank goodness for that. I didn't think I was ever so happy to learn that someone had a cat. "I've had her for a few years now. But never mind that. How can all of you be so wrong about how you hang your toilet paper?"

"What are you talking about?" Mildred asked. "Everyone knows toilet paper is supposed to be over, not under."

"Maybe let's get back to Hank," I said before things spiraled out of control via toilet paper wars. "What exactly did you two have a … disagreement about?" I almost said "fight," but if Hank could only respond by making the lights flicker on and off, I wasn't sure how much of a fight it could have been.

Ruth gave me an exasperated look. "I just told you. He put the toilet paper roll on wrong. Again. And I got upset, because it's been years at this point. He should know by now." Her face crumbled. "Now, it just seems so foolish. It was just a silly argument. Why would that cause him to leave?"

"Why indeed?" I murmured, even as I was still struggling to get my head around a ghost changing the toilet paper roll. Was that truly a thing? Even if a ghost could move things around, would any of them be using that power to change a toilet paper roll, or would they save it for things like rattling chains and slamming doors?

"I'm sure it's not forever," Aunt Tilde said, her brow creased with worry. "He probably just needed to blow off some steam or something. He'll be back."

"I don't think so," Ruth said, her chest starting to heave. Her coffee cup was rattling in its saucer, and Aunt Tilde took it from her. "I think he's really gone!"

"I'm sure that's not true," Aunt Tilde said. "Sometimes, people just need to walk away for a bit. To cool off."

"People do. Who knows, with ghosts," Mildred muttered under her breath, although it wasn't quiet enough to prevent Aunt Tilde or myself from hearing her. Aunt Tilde shot her a dark look.

"Hank doesn't do that though," Ruth said. "He's never done that, not once in all the years we've been together."

"Well, there's always a first," Aunt Tilde said. "I'm sure at any moment, he'll walk right through that front door and start … flicking the lights on and off again. And all will be well."

"I don't think so." Ruth finally got her breathing under control and straightened up. "This time, it's different."

"What's different about it?" Aunt Tilde asked.

"He …" Ruth swallowed hard, looking away as though she was losing her nerve. "He … left a message."

For the first time, Aunt Tilde looked slightly uneasy. "Message? What type of message?"

"A refrigerator-magnet message." Ruth's voice had dropped to nearly a whisper.

"What did it say?" Aunt Tilde matched her tone and volume.

Ruth hesitated, licking her lips. "It said … 'Bye.'"

And with that, she covered her face with her hands.

Chapter 3

For a moment, there was dead silence, apart from the sounds of Ruth's quiet sobbing. Even Mildred looked shaken.

"I'm sure it's nothing," Aunt Tilde said, patting Ruth on the shoulder. "People say bye all the time. It doesn't mean they're leaving for good."

"People, yes. Ghosts, no. At least, Hank never did," Ruth said, lifting her head out of her hands. Her eyes were red-rimmed, and her lipstick smeared, but otherwise, she seemed composed. "Hank never said anything like that. Nor did it ever seem like he left."

"What, you mean he was always with you?" Mildred asked.

"It wasn't like that," Ruth said crossly, giving her head a quick shake. She straightened up, smoothing out her blouse. "We weren't joined at the hip, if that's what you mean. He would do his thing, and I would do mine. Just like any married couple. Sometimes, he would be in the same room, and sometimes, he would be in different areas of the house ... but I always knew he was there, and I wasn't alone."

"So what's different about this?" Aunt Tilde asked, her voice soft.

Ruth chewed on her bottom lip. "It's hard to explain. There's just this ... emptiness. Like I know he isn't here. I can't smell him anymore. I always could before, even if he was in a different part of the house."

"Have you asked him any questions?" Mildred asked.

Ruth shot her a disgusted look. "Of course I have. What do you think? I've been asking over and over ..." her voice trailed off, and she squished up her face like she was going to start crying again.

"Of course you have. No one is blaming you." Aunt Tilde said, shooting Mildred another look. This time, I saw Mildred roll her eyes in response.

"Did anything else happen?" I asked. "When you thought he left, that is."

"I told you, he left the message on the fridge," Ruth said.

"Before that," I said. "You two were having your disagreement about the toilet paper roll, and then what happened? Did he walk out then, or what?"

She paused, thinking about my question. "I had just gotten home from the store. I was tired and in a bad mood." She made a face. "The checkout girl was so disrespectful. She called the manager before she even rang me up. It was so embarrassing."

Alarm bells filled my head, even though I wasn't sure why. "Why did she call the manager over?"

Ruth waved her hand. "Oh, I don't even know. Some silly misunderstanding with the bank. I had to promise I would call the bank, or they wouldn't let me take my groceries. Can you imagine?"

The alarm bells were turning into gongs. "No, that sounds terrible. Why would the bank do that?"

"Oh, who knows? It's these so-called computers, I tell you. They screw everything up. Mark my words; we're all going to rue the day we started relying on these contraptions. Anyway, I was in a terrible mood when I got home. I was starting to get one of my migraines … you know how I am when I get one of my migraines, Tilde?"

Tilde nodded, her face troubled. I wondered if she was hearing the alarms, as well. "I do."

"So once I got the groceries into the house, I immediately went to the bathroom, which was when I saw that the toilet paper roll was put on the wrong way. And I just … I just …" she squeezed her eyes together tightly and shook her head. "I just snapped at Hank. I shouldn't have. I see that now, but in that moment, I just felt like everything was on my shoulders. If I didn't do it, it didn't get done."

I bit my lip to keep from pointing out that if her spouse is a ghost, by definition, everything would be on her shoulders. Ruth was agitated enough, though. I didn't need to make things worse by bringing up reality.

"What did Hank say?" Aunt Tilde asked, sounding genuinely curious.

"He said he thought he had it right, but sometimes, it's difficult for him to tell," Ruth said. "According to Hank, being a ghost wreaks havoc on your spatial orientation."

"He said all of that?" Aunt Tilde asked, now sounding surprised. "How? Did he use the refrigerator magnets?"

Ruth shook her head. "No. I mean, he didn't really say all of that. But I knew that's what he wanted to say if he could, so I filled in the blanks. That's what happens when you've been married so long. It's like you can read each other's minds."

"Of course," Aunt Tilde said, nodding.

"But I was still so upset and irritated, I didn't want to hear any excuses, so I stayed in the bathroom. I took some aspirin and washed my face and rubbed my temples. The aspirin was just starting to kick in when I heard a door slam shut."

"Heavens, that must have given you a fright," Aunt Tilde asked.

Ruth started massaging her temples, as if reliving the bathroom scene. "Not really. Hank will sometimes slam a door, usually when he's frustrated about something. Or Sally will bat a door shut with her paws. Initially, I had thought it was just Hank letting me know he was unhappy with me. But it was a little strange, that time, because it sounded like the back door. Hank usually only slammed internal doors, not the ones to the outside. So I thought I'd better see what was going on. And that's when I found the message on the fridge."

"'Bye,'" Aunt Tilde said solemnly.

Ruth nodded. Her hands were clasped tightly together and resting in her lap, but I could see the tension in her forearms. "I rushed over to the back door, calling his name, hoping it wasn't the door I heard, but … I think it was."

"How could you tell?" Aunt Tilde asked.

She pressed her hands more tightly together. "The door was unlocked. And I never unlocked it, mostly because I almost never use it. So, if it was unlocked, that meant Hank must have unlocked it. And there was no reason for him to unlock it … unless he was leaving."

She looked up at us, and there was something so sad and vulnerable in her eyes, she somehow reminded me of a child, despite being more than twice my age.

"Why did he leave? It was just a silly fight," she said, her voice breaking. "He must have known I didn't mean it. It wasn't like it was our first fight, for heaven's sake. I don't understand."

"I'm sure he didn't leave because of the fight," Aunt Tilde said, reaching over to take Ruth's hand. "Maybe he just needed to get some air."

"Or maybe he went to get cigarettes," Mildred said, earning yet another glare from Aunt Tilde.

"He wouldn't have gotten cigarettes. He didn't smoke," Ruth said. "At least not anymore. And if he did start smoking again, he knows I would be very angry."

"That's probably why he hasn't come home yet," Mildred said. "He hasn't finished the pack."

Ruth looked horrified. "Oh, he better not be! He knows better. And to scare me like that over a smoke." She shook her head. "Of course I would forgive him, but we would definitely need to talk."

"Let's get back to Hank being missing," I said. While I didn't think there was much we could do about a missing ghost, I was sure there was absolutely nothing we could do about a ghost's smoking addiction. "You called us here because you want us to help you find him, right?"

She glanced up at me, blinking like she had forgotten I was even there, so lost in the unavoidable lecture she was going to give her husband's ghost about the evils of smoking. "Oh yes. Of course. That's what you do, right?" She turned to Aunt Tilde. "Your new detective agency. You find people. Right?"

"Right," Aunt Tilde said. "Among other things. 'Solving the un-solvable.' That's our motto."

"Oh, I love that!" Ruth's face broke out into a huge grin as she clapped her hands. "Solving the unsolvable. That's perfect."

I gritted my teeth. *Perfectly primed for someone to sue us,* I thought but didn't say. Luckily, Ruth wasn't waiting for an answer.

"You think you can find my Hank?" Ruth asked.

"I don't see why not," Aunt Tilde said briskly.

Wait, what? I had assumed we were going to gently explain how we weren't ghost hunters, but private investigators, and would not agree to look for a ghost. How was that even possible? I wanted to leap up and drag Aunt Tilde out of the room. Even Mildred looked taken aback.

"Um … it might be difficult to find a ghost," I said cautiously.

"I didn't say it would be easy, but nothing worthwhile is easy," Aunt Tilde said firmly.

Before I could reply to say I'd misspoke—I hadn't meant "difficult," but *impossible*, Ruth reached over and grasped Aunt Tilde's hand. "I can't tell you how relieved I am." She sounded close to tears. "I've been so alone these past two days. Sally is here, which does help, but every time I walk into a room, and I don't smell him, or I ask a question and don't get a response, the emptiness and loneliness practically overwhelm me." She swallowed hard. "I just … I just miss him so much."

"Of course you do," Aunt Tilde said, reaching over to squeeze her knee. "That's why we're going to do everything we can to find him. Okay?"

She nodded, her eyes glistening. Aunt Tilde smiled at her and gave her knee another squeeze.

All my objections died in my throat. I had no idea how we could possibly find a ghost, but I knew we had no choice but to try. "Um … do you think we can see the back door?"

Ruth swung her head over toward me, swiping at her eyes. "Of course. Obviously, you need to see the last place he was." She slowly and painfully pulled herself to her feet and started shuffling her way back to the hallway.

"Also, which bathroom were you in when you heard the door slam shut?" I asked, edging my coffee cup onto the coffee table. There wasn't a lot of room, with the pile of mail on one side and the tray on the other, but I managed to make it work. I stood up, flipping my notebook open just in time to see Aunt Tilde grinning at me as she gave me the thumbs-up sign. I hadn't quite decided if I was doing the right thing or not, as I was pretty sure this was all going to end badly, but clearly, this wasn't the time to share my concerns.

"It was this bathroom," Ruth said, gesturing toward a door in the hallway as she shuffled past. I glanced inside, noting it was a simple powder room with a toilet, sink, and medicine cabinet behind the mirror. It was decorated in blue and gold, although the gold was starting to tarnish. "I keep all my medications in that bathroom."

She continued down the hallway, but rather than turn toward the kitchen, she went down a different hallway, and then into a long, narrow room that doubled as both a mudroom and laundry room. The ancient washer and dryer were against one wall, while a jumble of shoes and books was on the other side. Next to the footwear was a coatrack, practically groaning under the weight of several coats, while next to the dryer was a long, low chest of drawers. The top was chipped and obviously used as a catch-all for a variety of odds and ends—a pile of library books, a small dish filled with an assortment of keys, several folded newspapers and flyers, a flashlight, and a couple of batteries.

Ruth waved toward the door. "This is it."

I followed Aunt Tilde and Mildred as they went to examine the door. It was plain, with no glass or decorations, painted brown, and looked heavy. Mildred reached for the doorknob and rattled it, but it didn't budge.

"See, it's locked. Just like I said," Ruth said.

"No, you said it wasn't locked," Mildred said, rattling the door again, as if her doing so would somehow magically open the door. "How did Hank get out if it was locked?"

"Normally, it is locked, just like it is now," Ruth said. "But when I checked after I heard the door slam shut, it wasn't."

"Did you look outside?" Mildred asked, still rattling the door as Aunt Tilde tried to turn the deadbolt. "To see if you could see where Hank went?"

Ruth gave her an exasperated look. "Of course I did."

"Did you see anything?" Mildred pressed as Aunt Tilde finally shoved her hand away from the doorknob, so she could unlock the door.

I assumed the answer would be no, but Ruth's expression turned pensive.

"I guess it depends on your definition of 'seeing,'" Ruth said.

Both Mildred and Aunt Tilde paused, as they turned to look at Ruth.

"You saw Hank?" Aunt Tilde asked.

Two bright-red circles appeared on Ruth's cheeks. "Well, no. I really don't *see* him. Not in this current evolution." I bit my cheek to keep from laughing. I suppose becoming a ghost could be considered something of an "evolution." "I'll sometimes see a blip or something from the corner of my eye. Usually when he's moving from one room to another. But ... oh, it's silly."

"No, it's not silly," Aunt Tilde said, taking a step toward Ruth. "You'd be amazed at what ends up being relevant, even if it doesn't seem like it could be now."

"Yes," Mildred chimed in. "A lot of times, it's the smallest details that end up cracking a case."

"Well," Ruth said, swallowing hard. Her hands were fluttering near her sides. "It's just ..." She broke off, taking a deep breath. I thought she might start crying again, but her eyes were dry.

"What, Ruth?" I asked gently. I was the one closest to her, so I reached out to put a hand on her arm. Her skin felt dry and papery thin. And cold. So cold. Which made no sense, considering how suffocating warm her house was. "What did you see?"

She swallowed again and met my gaze. Her eyes were watery behind her glasses. "I saw Hank." Her voice dropped to nearly a whisper.

I shivered. Despite the stuffiness of her house, the cold from her hand had somehow traveled to my spine, making goosebumps rise on my back. "What do you mean, you saw him?" I asked. "You said you never saw him."

She twirled one hand next to her head. "It was like what I normally saw. That ... that flicker of movement. I saw it for sure."

I stared at her, horror starting to creep up my spine. "There was someone in your backyard?"

She shook her head firmly. "I saw *Hank*. Not just any someone."

I let go of her arm and eased my way between Mildred and Aunt Tilde, so I could open the back door. "Describe what you saw," I said as I twisted the knob. The door was heavier than I thought, which surprised me. Apparently, Ruth was stronger than I gave her credit for.

"It was over there," Ruth said, waving vaguely to her right as she came closer to me. Aunt Tilde and Mildred, both uncharacteristically silent, moved to let her pass. I wrenched the door open and stepped outside onto the cracked cement stoop.

Even though it was still fairly warm and humid out, the air was so much cooler than in Ruth's house. I took a deep breath, inhaling the scent of pine needles and weeds. The yard was a mess of grass that really needed to be cut, dandelions, and overgrown bushes.

"So over there?" I asked, waving toward the right side of the house. There was a row of tall pines and old oak trees lining the yard.

Ruth stood in the doorway. "I stepped out, just like you did, and from the corner of my eye, I saw a flash. I turned my head, but whatever it was had disappeared around the corner. I …" she swallowed again. "I called Hank's name, but there was no answer."

"Did you walk around the house?" I asked.

She shook her head. "Although I did go to the front door and searched the yard out there." I could already see from her face that she hadn't seen anything.

I went back to studying the yard. It was basically an unkempt jungle, so who knew if someone had been out there or not?

"It doesn't mean he's not coming back," Aunt Tilde said quietly from behind Ruth.

"Exactly," Mildred said briskly. "Once he finishes his cigarettes, I'm sure he'll be back."

Ruth was starting to look like it was all she could do to hold back tears, but her expression changed to indignation with Mildred's comment. "It can't be that. How long does it take to smoke a pack of cigarettes? Certainly not two days."

"You don't know that," Mildred said. "By your count, he hasn't had a cigarette in, what? Over a decade?"

"At least," Ruth said before muttering under her breath, "It better be longer than that."

"Well, he's out of practice," Mildred said. "There's no way he can smoke a cigarette as fast as he used to. Plus, he's a ghost now, so who knows how long it might take? And maybe he got a few packs. You just don't know."

Ruth frowned. "I guess so. You may have a point."

"Of course I have a point," Mildred said triumphantly.

I made my way back into the stuffy house and shut the door behind me, noticing how stiff the hinges were. "Do you ever use this door?"

"Not a lot," she said. "I usually use the garage door."

"So after you called Hank's name, what did you do?"

"I came back inside and went to the front of the house to see if I could catch him," Ruth said. "But there was nothing there."

"Did you see anything at all?"

She shook her head. "Nothing unusual. Someone taking a walk down the street and a couple of cars on the road."

Someone taking a walk? My instincts immediately perked up and went straight to high-alert mode. "Who was the person walking? Did you recognize him?"

"It was a her, and no, but I only saw her from the back," Ruth said. She gestured toward her head. "A lot of brown hair. It wasn't anyone I recognized."

My instincts deflated a bit, although there was really no reason for it. A woman could have broken into her house as easily as a man. But if Ruth thought whoever she was seeing was her dead husband, it made sense she had seen a man instead of a woman, so it probably wasn't related.

"So, after you checked the front of the house, what did you do?" I asked.

"I started searching all the rooms. I couldn't believe Hank would have left me, not over such a silly argument! I figured he was probably just not answering me because he was irritated and wanted to teach me a lesson." Her shoulders slumped. "That's what I kept telling myself, anyway. But even as I was searching, I knew. I could feel it in my gut that there was something different this time … something wrong … and then I found the message on the fridge. And just like that, it was ten years ago, and I had lost him all over again." She turned to Aunt Tilde, her face stricken. "What am I going to do? How am I going to live without him?"

Chapter 4

Ruth's chest was heaving, although her eyes remained dry and her breathing was strained. Aunt Tilde stepped forward to take her arm, her expression concerned.

"Maybe we should go back to the living room and sit down," Aunt Tilde said.

Ruth nodded and let Aunt Tilde lead her back to the living room, while Mildred and I trailed after them. I could hear Aunt Tilde murmur something to Ruth, but I couldn't make out the actual words. Not that I was listening. My head was too busy spinning as I tried to make sense of it. Not that I believed in ghosts, missing or otherwise, but if Hank wasn't the cause of the slamming doors, flickering lights, and botched replacement of toilet paper rolls, then who was? There was apparently a cat in the house, and while it was possible a cat would slam a door or turn a light on and off, I didn't think it would be able to change a toilet paper roll or leave a coherent refrigerator-magnet message.

Was someone sneaking into Ruth's house? Just the thought of that was enough to give me the creeps, but what would be the point? To gaslight an old, lonely woman? That just sounded evil, but what other reason could there be? Maybe they were also stealing from her. I would have to ask Ruth if she was missing any items, especially anything expensive.

There was another explanation, but in a way, it was even worse than someone sneaking in. What if Ruth herself was doing it? But if it was her, was she doing it on purpose? Or did she not even know she was doing it? I studied Ruth's frail shoulders as Aunt Tilde helped her back down into her chair. She seemed coherent and mentally "with it," but that didn't mean there wasn't something wrong with her.

And if she was suffering from dementia or some other medical condition … I glanced around the room as I made my way back to where I'd been sitting before. Like the rest of the house, it was mostly neat, but not necessarily clean. Dust was everywhere, along with telltale strands of cat hair scattered all over the carpet. Of course, just because she wasn't cleaning regularly didn't mean there was anything wrong with her. Maybe she just didn't like to clean.

But … it was still a lot of house for one person. Especially one who seemed so alone in the world.

"I'm so sorry to make such a fuss," Ruth said as her hands fluttered over the coffeepot, refilling cups. "I'm not usually like this."

"There's nothing to apologize for," Aunt Tilde said. "Of course you're a wreck. Who wouldn't be?"

"Do you have anyone who might come stay with you?" I asked softly as Ruth leaned over to top off my coffee cup. "I'm not trying to overstep, but maybe you shouldn't be alone right now."

Ruth's hand twitched, sloshing the coffee onto the table and some of the mail stacked next to my cup. "Oh heavens, I'm such a klutz," she said, the pot trembling as she tried to set it down. "I didn't get any on you, did I?"

"No, I'm fine. I've got it, don't worry about it," I said, grabbing a handful of napkins and mopping up the mess.

Ruth watched me, wringing her hands. "I should get a washcloth. That's not your job."

"Nonsense, we're happy to help. I can get the washcloth," Aunt Tilde said, getting to her feet, but Mildred put a hand on her arm to stop her.

"Actually, let me help Emily," Mildred said as she headed out of the living room.

"Oh, you don't have to do that," Ruth said. She seemed frozen, glued to the same spot, still wringing her hands. "You're a guest. I should be taking care of you."

"We're friends," Aunt Tilde said, reaching over to clasp her hands. "We're here to help you, not to cause more work for you."

"Besides, I should be moving around more," Mildred announced as she returned with a wet washcloth. "I get stiff if I sit for too long. You're doing me a favor."

That got a small smile from Ruth.

"But Emily has a good point," Aunt Tilde continued as both she and Ruth sat down. I picked up the stack of mail to try to wipe the worst of the coffee off while Mildred wiped down the table. "Do you have anyone to help you?"

"Lynne comes by every few days to check on me and Hank," Ruth said.

"Lynne Anderson? Oh, of course. I forgot she lives near you," Aunt Tilde said.

"Right across the street," Ruth said. "Been there for years. I don't know what I would have done without her."

Aunt Tilde looked stricken. "I'm so sorry. I should have stopped by more."

"Oh hush," Ruth said, shaking her head. "You are absolutely fine. I don't need a babysitter. I'm perfectly capable of taking care of myself, and between Hank, Lynn, and Bradley, everything was covered."

"Bradley?" Aunt Tilde asked, a slight crease between her eyes. "I don't think I know a Bradley."

"Oh, he's been such a help. Especially around the yard. I don't know what I would have done without him either," Ruth said.

I had been trying to save a drenched envelope, but the yard reference caused me to look up. Had she seen her backyard? Man, I hoped she wasn't paying him for his "help."

"Do you remember his last name?" Aunt Tilde asked.

Ruth paused and furrowed her brow. "I'm sure he told me at one point, but now I can't remember."

"How did you meet him?" Aunt Tilde asked.

"He was friends with Hank. Or maybe he worked with him. I can't recall exactly." Ruth flapped one of her hands. "He came by a few years ago, wanted to see if he could help out. Said he couldn't stop thinking about me and wanted to make sure Hank's widow was taken care of the way Hank would have wanted." She smiled, an almost dreamy smile.

I gave up on the soaked envelope and started peeling its contents out of it, hoping I could at least save that. I paused, feeling uncomfortable. At the same time, I reasoned, the envelope was already open. It wasn't like I was opening her mail, exactly. I studied the envelope again. It looked like it was some sort of official government correspondence, though it was likely simply junk mail disguised as official. Just thinking about it was enough to make my blood boil. Ruth was precisely the type of person who might be fooled by a scam like that.

"Ruth, I'm so sorry, but this envelope is kind of destroyed." I held it up. "But it looks like the letter is fine. Is it important? It appears it might be from the state of Wisconsin." I was hoping my not-so-subtle method of figuring out whether the letter was legit or not would work. And if it wasn't legit, my next step would be determining how caught up in the scam she was.

Ruth's eyes suddenly got very big. "Oh, that. That's nothing." Her hands fluttered in front of her. "Don't worry about that. I've got it handled."

"Are you sure?" I asked. I was trying not to look at it, but out of the corner of my eye, I noticed a lot of scary words, such as Final Notice, You Owe Us Back Taxes, and Contact Us by August 15.

And that brought to light an even bigger problem: it was already past August 15. Did that mean she had already been scammed?

"Yes, yes. It's fine," Ruth said.

"But it says you owe back taxes," Mildred said.

"What?" Aunt Tilde yelped, staring at Ruth, who had a bright-red flush creeping up her neck. "You didn't pay your property taxes?"

"Of course I've paid my taxes," Ruth said. "I always pay my taxes. It's just a misunderstanding is all."

Mildred snatched the letter from my hand. "This doesn't look like a misunderstanding. It looks like the state of Wisconsin is going to take your house."

"Oh no. That's not going to happen," Ruth said.

"How do you know?" Mildred asked. "Did you talk to them?"

"Well, no," Ruth said. "But I'm sure they won't take my home. I've lived here my entire adult life. Hank and I moved here right after we were married. The state wouldn't take my home away from me."

"They will if you don't pay your taxes," Mildred said.

"Have you been paying your taxes?" Aunt Tilde asked.

"Well, of course," Ruth said.

"Then why does the state of Wisconsin say you haven't?" Mildred asked.

"It's probably just some sort of mix-up. You know how the government can be. All that bureaucratic red tape. I'm sure someone just misfiled something," Ruth said.

Mildred was skimming the letter. "Even if someone misfiled a payment, you have to contact them."

"I will. I told you, I've got it handled," Ruth said.

Mildred looked up and narrowed her eyes. "You're absolutely sure you paid?"

"Yes! How many times do I have to tell you? I pay my taxes," Ruth said, her tone exasperated.

"You paid? Or did Hank?"

Ruth's face seemed to freeze. She tried to say something but erupted in a coughing fit instead.

Mildred was staring at her in horror. "Oh no. Please don't tell me you put your dead husband in charge of paying your taxes."

"Of course I didn't," Ruth said with a sniff. "How would that even work? He can't write a check."

Hank couldn't write a check, but he could leave refrigerator-magnet messages and apparently also change the toilet paper roll. I vowed then and there to someday have someone explain ghost physics to me.

If anything, Mildred looked even more horrified. "You had someone else writing checks for you?"

Ruth looked put out. "Why would you think such a thing? Of course I didn't. I always write my own checks."

"Did you write a check for the property taxes?"

"Yes, yes. Of course I did." But she had stopped making eye contact, and there was an unreadable expression on her face. "I must have," she added quietly.

Aunt Tilde closed her eyes. "Oh, Ruth. What did you do?"

"I didn't do anything," Ruth said. Her expression shifted again, and now she looked like a cornered rat. "I'm sure I paid my taxes. I remember writing the check and giving it to Bradley to mail-"

"Bradley again," Aunt Tilde cut in. "Who is this Bradley person?"

"I told you. He helps me with the yard."

"You're having the gardener pay your property taxes?" Mildred asked.

"You do know gardeners make horrible accountants," Aunt Tilde said. "Remember that gardener Jacklyn hired that one time? It was such a mess. Never once did he give her a correct invoice. It was always too much or too little. Drove her crazy."

"I thought Jacklyn hired a landscaper, not a gardener," Mildred said.

"No, he was a gardener. I'm sure of it," Aunt Tilde said.

"I'm pretty sure he was a landscaper," Mildred said. "Remember, he wanted to dig up all her beautiful old oak trees and build a garage there instead. It didn't even make sense, as he'd have to put a driveway straight through her rose bushes."

"You're thinking of that dreadful contractor her husband hired," Aunt Tilde said. "Her husband was the one who wanted to build a huge workshop right in the middle of their front yard. Would have been a terrible eyesore. Luckily, Jacklyn was able to veto that in time." She frowned. "Now that I think about it, that contractor screwed up his invoices, as well."

"Oh, contractors are the worst at accounting," Mildred said. "Definitely don't have them pay your taxes."

"But I didn't have a contractor pay my taxes," Ruth said.

"That's right … you had your gardener pay your taxes, not your contractor," Aunt Tilde said.

"No, that's not right," Ruth said. "I said Bradley mailed the check for me, not that he paid it. He was always helpful like that. Mailing checks for me, running errands, doing stuff outside of the house. It wasn't like I could ask Hank to help me with those sorts of things. I didn't even think Hank could leave the house until two days ago." She dabbed at her eyes as she shook her head. "We're definitely going to have a long talk about a lot of things, if he comes back."

"I still think it's a bad idea to hire a gardener to do your accounting," Mildred said. "And for the record, I think it would also be a bad idea to ask Hank to mail checks or run errands for you."

"Like I said, we have a lot to talk about," Ruth said.

"Are you sure he put the checks in the mail?" I asked, hoping to keep the conversation from derailing even further than it already had. There were all sorts of alarm bells ringing in my head over this Bradley guy, and it wasn't just because of the terrible job he did on her yard.

Ruth gave me a puzzled look. "What else would he do with them? They were in an envelope."

"Were they stamped?" Mildred asked.

Ruth crossed her arms over her chest and gave Mildred a hard look. "What are you saying? You think there's something so wrong with me that I would forget a stamp?"

"I don't think anything is wrong with you. People forget things all the time," Mildred said. "All I'm trying to do is figure out why the state of Wisconsin is saying you haven't paid property taxes for three years."

Ruth's eyes nearly bugged out of her head. "Three years?" Her skin had drained of color, turning chalky white.

Aunt Tilde's eyes also went wide, and she pressed a hand against her mouth. "Ruth, what have you done?"

Ruth started shaking her head uncontrollably. "That can't be right. It can't be."

"That's why the state can take your home," Mildred said, shaking the letter. "According to this letter, they've been sending you multiple notices about you owing back taxes, and because you haven't responded, they're getting ready to foreclose on your home."

"What? No, that's not true," Ruth said, getting more and more agitated. "Of course I paid. I wouldn't have not paid my taxes for three years!"

Mildred shook the letter again. "But that's what the letter says. Didn't you read it?"

"Well, obviously, I read it," Ruth said. "They must have put all of that in the fine print. You know I can't read all that small lettering anymore, yet everyone insists on making things as tiny as possible."

"I agree, it's so frustrating trying to read anything anymore," Aunt Tilde said. "Everything is way too small. All these companies should be ashamed of themselves for making their correspondence so difficult to read."

"This is in bold and large type," Mildred said.

There was an awkward silence. Mildred was busy biting her bottom lip, probably because she was just itching to ask Ruth if Hank was the one who had read the letter and not her. Luckily, even she realized how bad everything was for Ruth.

"All right, I didn't read it," Ruth said. She collapsed onto the chair, her shoulders slumping. "Not really. I just kind of ..." She waved her hands at the letter. "I don't know, skimmed it."

"Why, Ruth?" Aunt Tilde's voice was gentle. "Why didn't you at least read it? It's from the state of Wisconsin. You must have known it was important."

Ruth stared at her hands. "I thought it was being taken care of." Her voice dropped to a whisper. "Bradley said he was taking care of it. He was taking care of it!" She raised her head and looked between us, her voice becoming more plaintive. "He said he was taking care of it. He wouldn't lie to me. He wouldn't."

Chapter 5

"Maybe you need to start at the beginning," Aunt Tilde said. Her voice was still gentle, but there was a cold, hard edge to it. No one messed with Aunt Tilde's friends. "You said Bradley just showed up one day and said he knew Hank?"

Ruth nodded, but she still didn't look up. "He was friends with Hank. Or they worked together. I don't remember now."

"When was this?"

"I don't know. At least a few years ago. I was having some health challenges at the time, I remember that ... and I was really struggling to get stuff done around the house. Lynne, bless her soul, was a huge help, but she has her own life. She couldn't be showing up here every day to take care of an old lady. I had looked into hiring someone, one of those caregivers who help with cooking and cleaning—not a nurse—but even that was so expensive. Hank told me I should do it anyway." A faint smile touched her lips. "He said I was absolutely worth it. But he didn't realize how difficult things had been for me since he was gone. I mean, he did what he could, and just having him in the house made such a huge difference for me. But ..." she paused and gave her head a quick shake before looking up at us, her eyes huge and pleading. "He did his best, but being a ghost is just ... well, it's different. He doesn't have the same concerns we do." She gestured between us. "Ghosts don't eat. They don't get warm or cold. They don't need clothes. They have no use for money, and even though he knows money is important and that I need it to pay for everything I need to live, after a while, when you don't need to pay for things, I think you just ... forget."

"Maybe he should have quit using up the toilet paper then," Mildred said. "It's not like he needed it. And toilet paper costs good money."

"Well." Ruth seemed a bit flustered. "Some habits die hard. And I think he kept a few of them to just feel, human, I suppose."

I didn't even want to know what a ghost was doing with toilet paper that was making him feel human.

"But Hank did a good job taking care of you," Aunt Tilde said. "When he was alive, I mean. Obviously, he did what he could as a ghost. But when he was alive, he set you up financially, didn't he?"

Ruth hesitated. "I thought he had. And I think he thought he had. He often told me he had a plan, and if something happened to him, he was going to make sure I never had to worry about money, but …" She twisted her hands together in her lap. "Our savings weren't as … robust as I had hoped. And after all the … unpleasantness, the company he worked for ended up giving me a settlement, rather than his full pension."

Unpleasantness? I opened my mouth to ask, but Aunt Tilde caught my eye and gave me a quick headshake. I closed my mouth.

"A settlement?" Mildred asked, aghast. "They had no reason to do that. You should have gotten his full pension. Hank earned that!"

Ruth wrung her hands together tighter. "I know. I couldn't believe how terribly they treated me. Especially after all those years Hank worked for them."

"You should have hired a lawyer and sued them," Mildred said.

Ruth hung her head. "I tried. I talked to a lawyer, who was very kind, but he told me it wasn't worth it. Even if I won, it would be a long, brutal battle that could bankrupt me in the process. He agreed it wasn't fair, and the company shouldn't have done what it did to me, but said it was better for me to take the settlement. So I did."

"Oof. Lawyers." Mildred sat back in her seat, folding her arms over her chest and throwing me an icy look like, like the whole thing was somehow my fault. "They're all the same. Worthless."

"Not all of them," Aunt Tilde chimed in before I could say anything. I assumed Mildred was referring to Nick Stewart, who was (unofficially) The Redemption Detective Agency's lawyer. However, like everyone else besides me, he wasn't getting paid, so I wasn't sure if we could call him that. And to add another plot twist, even though Nick was dating Trisha, and I was dating Jerome, Mildred wanted to make sure Nick and I didn't end up together. I had told her multiple times it wouldn't happen, but she never seemed convinced.

"All. Of. Them," Mildred said again, her tone dark. She transferred her icy glare to Aunt Tilde, who rolled her eyes in response.

"But despite all of that, I was able to make ends meet," Ruth continued. "It wasn't easy, especially since I couldn't talk to Hank about it. I knew it would upset him if he knew what had happened with his pension, so I just did what I could. But when it came time to see about hiring some extra help, it just wasn't in the budget. So, you can imagine how happy I was when Bradley knocked on my door."

"Wait. Bradley just showed up out of nowhere and offered to help you?" Aunt Tilde asked, disbelief dripping from her words, although she tried to hide it by softening her tone.

"I offered to pay him," Ruth insisted, a flush staining her too-pale cheeks. "I couldn't offer much, but that didn't end up mattering, because he refused. Said Hank had always been nice to him, and he wanted to pay that kindness back by helping me out. It started with him doing the yard work. He would come by at least once a week to mow the lawn and trim the weeds. And then he started asking if he could pick up some groceries for me before he came by. I was so relieved to have someone shopping for me, so of course I said yes. And as the post office is right by the grocery store, he offered to drop off my bills or anything else I needed to mail. It made perfect sense for him to do that if he was going to be at the grocery store anyway." Her eyes shifted as she looked from each one of us, her gaze beseeching. "Bradley wouldn't have done anything to hurt me. He was always so nice to me. This must be some sort of misunderstanding."

Mildred was still biting her bottom lip. At this point, she had practically chewed off her bright-pink lipstick completely, and Aunt Tilde had started massaging her temples. Neither of them made any move to say anything, so I decided to jump in.

"You know, the state sends out multiple notices before something like this happens," I said gently. "What happened when you got the initial notices? Did you ask Bradley about them?"

"Bradley told me he would take care of it," Ruth said, her voice hollow. She pressed her fingers above her eyes, shaking her head slowly. "What am I going to do? I can't lose my home."

Mildred held a hand up. "Wait a minute—Bradley knew? You actually told him?" She sounded incredulous, as if she couldn't believe she was having this conversation.

"Of course I told him. Why wouldn't I? He was helping me with my finances." A defensive tone had crept into Ruth's voice.

Mildred's jaw dropped. "He was *helping* you with your finances? Not just mailing your checks?"

Aunt Tilde closed her eyes. "Oh, Ruth."

"I …" Ruth stared at us, her eyes frantically shifting from one face to another. "You don't understand," she cried out, the words bursting from her like they had been trapped for too long. "It was just so difficult after Hank died. He had always taken care of the bills. My job was to take care of the house, and I thought … I thought he was happy with me. I always made his favorite meals. I made sure the house was clean and welcoming when he came home. I don't know what I did wrong."

"You didn't do anything wrong," Aunt Tilde said quickly. She cut her eyes toward Mildred, as if daring her to say anything, but Mildred appeared to be refocused on chewing on her bottom lip. "Hank loved you. It was all a misunderstanding."

"That's what I told myself," Ruth said. "There was just a big misunderstanding, and the cops would eventually sort it out. But they never did."

Cops? My eyes widened, but now Aunt Tilde was giving me a hard look, so I also kept my mouth shut. The one I got from Mildred, then, was sympathetic.

"There was so much I didn't know," Ruth continued. "I had never balanced a checkbook before. I didn't even know all the bills I had to pay. It was just so overwhelming. And then I … and then I …" she broke off and dropped her gaze to her lap.

"And then you what?" Aunt Tilde asked gently, squeezing her hand.

Ruth shook her head but didn't lift her eyes. "It's just so embarrassing," she said, her voice so low I had to strain to hear her. "I bounced a check at the grocery store. I had never done that before. I was so mortified."

"Oh, that's nothing to be embarrassed about," Aunt Tilde said. "Heavens, one of my coworkers once forgot to make any of her car payments. Now that was embarrassing. Especially when the cops showed up at the hospital. It was quite the spectacle."

"Wait, the cops were doing repo work?" I asked, even as a part of me screamed to keep my mouth shut, so we didn't go down yet another rabbit hole.

Mildred rolled her eyes. "No, the cops weren't doing repo work. I heard she had taken the car for a test drive and never returned it."

"That's because she went to a dealership in Illinois," Aunt Tilde said. "Or maybe it was Iowa."

"I heard it was Indiana," Mildred said.

Aunt Tilde waved her hand. "Well, it was one of those 'I' states. Wherever it was, it was a long drive. You can't expect her to turn right around and come back the same day."

"Maybe she should have thought about that before choosing that dealership," Mildred said. "She could have gone somewhere closer, like Riverview."

"No, I don't think she could have," Aunt Tilde said. "I'm pretty sure it was a Riverview dealership that kicked her out and told her if she showed up again, they'd call the cops on her. Horrible customer service, if you ask me."

"Maybe she took one of their cars on a 'test drive' and didn't return it." Mildred made air quotes around the words "test drive."

"Well, in her defense, it can be confusing when the dealership tells you to take all of the time that you need," Aunt Tilde said. "Sometimes, it takes a few days to decide if a car is right for you."

"Or, in her case, a few months," Mildred said

"Well, it was also hard to shift into gear," Aunt Tilde said. "It was sticky or something. She was trying to see if she could work it out."

I pressed my lips together. No, I wasn't going to ask why she didn't just return it to the dealer if that were the case. We were way off-track as it was. "So, did you ask Bradley to help you with the bounced check?" I asked Ruth, who had been watching the exchange between Aunt Tilde and Mildred with wide eyes. Her eyes shifted to me, as that bright-red flush returned to her cheeks.

"I didn't know what to do," she said, her voice low. "Nothing like that had ever happened to me before. It sounds so silly when I say it out loud like this. But at the time …" her voice trailed off.

I leaned toward her. "I totally get it. The first time I wrote a check, I didn't do it right, and I had to tear it up and write a new one. I was so mortified, I wanted to crawl in a hole."

That surprised her. She jerked her head up to look at me. "Really?"

I nodded. Out of the corner of my eye, I saw Aunt Tilde frown in disgust as she mouthed her sister's, my mother's, name. There was a reason why I always had a soft spot for Aunt Tilde, despite how different we were. "No one had ever taught me how to open a bank account or write a check. I had to learn to do it all myself, and it was really hard at first."

"There's no instruction guide or anything," Ruth said.

"I know. You'd think they would give you something at the bank when you open an account. Like a little handout or something."

Ruth's eyes brightened. "Exactly. They make it so confusing." She leaned forward as well, keeping her gaze steady on mine, like she was confessing something truly awful—like not returning a car she had been test-driving for weeks. "I was way too embarrassed to ask Lynne, and there was no one else I could turn to. I wouldn't have told Bradley either, but he was here working on the yard when the bank called. I had just gotten off the phone when he knocked on the door. He had a question about the yard, I think … I can't remember now, but he took one look at my face and knew something had happened. He refused to leave until I told him what. He was so sweet." Her face crumbled at the memory. "He told me it was no big deal; practically everyone bounced a check at some point in their life. He helped me fix it and explained what I needed to do so it wouldn't happen again. But it was so confusing and overwhelming, and I was scared I would do it again, so that's when he started helping me."

"And when exactly was that?" I kept my voice as gentle as I could, even as the anger was building inside me. This sweet, naïve woman had been completely taken advantage of by a horrible con artist. Mildred was looking like she too was struggling to hold back her anger, but Aunt Tilde just looked ill. "Was it three years ago?"

She paused for a moment, thinking. "It's so hard to remember exactly, but yeah, I think so." Her eyes focused on me. "But Bradley couldn't have done this. He was so nice and helpful. I'm sure it's just a misunderstanding with the government. The government is always messing something up."

"Is that what Bradley told you?" I asked, keeping my voice gentle.

She hesitated before nodding. "He said he would take care of it for me. Told me not to worry about it. 'These things happen all the time,' he said. I was relieved, of course, and happy to let him deal with the state."

"Do you remember getting any other notices?" I asked.

She screwed up her face. "At least one more. I remember he got really upset, told me he couldn't believe they still hadn't fixed it, but that I shouldn't worry, he would take care of it for me. He would go down there the very next day and give them a piece of his mind. He said they should be ashamed of themselves for scaring me like that."

I nodded toward the notice in Mildred's hand. "What about that one?"

She bit her lip. "I was sure it was just another mix-up. I was waiting to see Bradley, so I could ask him."

"Wait, Bradley doesn't know about that notice?" I asked.

She shook her head. "I haven't seen him in a while. I've been worried about him. I hope he's alright."

All the alarm bells had started going off in my head again. "When was the last time you saw him?"

She furrowed her brow. "Four or five months ago? It's hard for me to keep track."

The alarms grew louder. I was trying to keep my expression neutral because I didn't want to upset Ruth more than she already was. "Did he tell you he wasn't going to be around?"

She gave me a faintly exasperated look. "Of course. I told you, I'm sure this is all a big misunderstanding. Bradley wouldn't do anything to hurt me on purpose. He told me he had to go home to see his sister. He was having some family issues, and his sister needed him. But he was so worried about leaving me. He kept asking if I would be alright, and I told him of course I would be, and he needed to be there for his family."

"Have you tried to contact him?" I asked.

Ruth started plucking at her pants, as if she was trying to get specks of dust off of them. I suspected it was really just a side effect of her anxiety. "I can't. I don't have a phone number for him."

"But what about here in Redemption? Have you tried calling him here?" I asked.

Pluck. Pluck. Pluck. "He never gave me his phone number."

"He never gave you a phone number?" Mildred burst out, almost as if she could no longer contain the words inside her. "Didn't you ask?"

"There was no need." Her plucking became more frantic. "He was always showing up. I didn't have to call him."

"But did you ask?" Mildred pressed. Aunt Tilde shot her a hard look, but Mildred ignored her.

"I did, once, but he told me he was in the process of moving, so the number would probably change. He told me he'd give it to me once he was settled somewhere," Ruth said. She wasn't looking at anyone, maybe because she was realizing how she sounded. "I know he was having a tough time finding a place to rent. He told me multiple times that there were a lot of shady characters out there, and it was difficult to find a decent landlord. I would have asked him to stay with me, but …" she hesitated, still not making eye contact. "Well, it doesn't matter."

"Of course it matters," Aunt Tilde finally said. "Did he want to move in with you?"

She squirmed in her seat. "Maybe. He hinted a lot about it. But I wasn't comfortable with him living here. Hank was here with me … I don't know. I was afraid that if Bradley were here, I wouldn't be able to talk to Hank anymore."

Well, chalk one up for the ghost. I suspected it would have been a disaster if Bradley had moved in with her. He probably would have stolen even more than he had from her, but luckily, Hank protected her from that.

"Where is his family from?" I asked. Maybe if we at least knew that, the cops could try to locate him. Although without a last name, I wasn't sure how successful they would be.

She thought about it for a minute. "Somewhere in Minnesota. Or maybe it was Michigan."

"Or, heck, maybe it was Milwaukee," Mildred said. Aunt Tilde glared at her.

"But I'm sure he'll be in touch again," Ruth said firmly. "Once he's back in Redemption, I mean. I'm sure whatever was going on with his family just took longer than he thought, but once he sorts that out, he'll come back and take care of this mess." Her voice was surprisingly confident, almost as if she hadn't been paying attention to the last half-hour of our conversation.

Aunt Tilde, Mildred, and I exchanged glances. Aunt Tilde was the one who spoke. "Honey," she said, putting her hand on Ruth's hand. "He's not going to be in touch."

Ruth snatched her hand away. "Of course he is. You'll see." Her voice rose an octave. "It's just a misunderstanding. Bradley has got this under control. He just needs to go talk to the state."

"No, he doesn't," Aunt Tilde said. Her voice was compassionate, but there was a steel edge that I remembered from childhood when I did something that displeased her. "He's not going to be in touch because he was the one who made this mess."

Ruth's jaw dropped. "No! What are you saying? Bradley didn't do this. It was the government! Bradley would never hurt me."

Aunt Tilde simply squeezed her hand harder. "Ruth, I'm just so sorry."

Something in Aunt Tilde's voice must have finally cracked through Ruth's denial, because she covered her face and wept.

Chapter 6

The rest of the conversation was even more of a mess, if such a thing were even possible.

Even after Ruth got herself under control, she continued to insist this was all a massive misunderstanding, and once the government went through their records, they would find all of her checks.

"I sent them, and they were cashed, so they have to have them," she kept saying.

Even when Mildred told her the reason why they were cashed was likely because Bradley cashed them, she insisted that couldn't be the case. "I wrote them to the State of Wisconsin. How could Bradley cash a check that wasn't written to him?"

I briefly tried to explain that scammers had ways to alter checks so they could cash them, but then Aunt Tilde interjected with a story about one of her friends whose cousin was a con artist with a whole roofing company scam going, except Mildred was sure it wasn't a roofing scam, but that he was actually roofing people with the date rape drug in order to blackmail them. Ruth then insisted she had never been drugged. Besides, Bradley would never do that to her or anyone.

"Why don't we simply call the state of Wisconsin and ask them about your taxes?" I suggested.

Ruth's eyes went wide. "Oh, we can't do that. We have to wait for Bradley."

I briefly closed my eyes. "Why do we have to wait for Bradley?"

"Because he's been dealing with them. He'll know who to talk to and what to do."

I was starting to despair. I had no idea how to convince her before it was too late, and she lost her home.

But then Aunt Tilde chimed in. "Yes, but we don't know where Bradley is. And what if something happened to him? Then what? We need to respond to this now."

Ruth gasped. "Something happened to Bradley? No, that can't possibly be right. He's young. I'm sure he's fine. He's just taking care of his family."

"How do you know?" Aunt Tilde challenged. "You haven't seen him in months. Has Bradley ever done that to you before?"

Ruth shook her head. "No, he's always been very dependable."

"So that sounds to me like something happened to him," Aunt Tilde said.

"But what about his family?" Ruth asked.

Aunt Tilde held her hands up. "What about them? Maybe his family is taking more time and energy than he initially thought, and he won't return to Redemption for six more months? In the meantime, you'll have lost your home."

Ruth let out a strangled squeak and pressed a hand against her chest. "No, no, that can't happen." All the blood had drained from her face, and she was shaking her head violently. I was suddenly very concerned she was going to have a heart attack and leaned forward. Aunt Tilde seemed to have the same thought because she grasped Ruth's arm. "I can't lose my home! That can't happen."

"I know. That's why we need to call the government-" Aunt Tilde started to say, but Ruth made that strange noise again.

"No, you don't understand," Ruth said. Her eyes were filling with tears. "I can't lose my home. What if Hank comes back? He won't be able to find me! I can't leave! I *won't* leave."

"And you won't have to," Aunt Tilde said firmly.

I gaped at her. "Wait, what?" *We can't possibly promise that,* I wanted to shout, but I eyed Ruth and closed my mouth.

Ruth's breathing had started to calm down, and the color was returning to her cheeks. "I won't?"

"No." Aunt Tilde leaned forward to squeeze Ruth's hand. "This is your home, yours and Hank's, and if you don't want to leave, you won't have to."

"Um, Aunt Tilde, can I … speak with you? Privately?" I asked, gesturing with my head toward the kitchen.

Aunt Tilde straightened up and clutched Ruth's hand harder. "There's nothing you can say to me privately that you can't say here."

Oh geez. I slumped down in my seat. We were absolutely going to get sued one of these days.

At least Ruth looked almost normal again, so if nothing else, Aunt Tilde had kept her from having to go to the hospital. "How are you going to do that?"

"We're going to take your case, that's how," Aunt Tilde said triumphantly.

Ruth's eyes went wide. "Take my case? You mean your detective agency?"

"That's exactly what I mean," Aunt Tilde said. "We're going to get to the bottom of what's going on with your property taxes, so you don't need to worry anymore."

"Oh." Ruth swallowed. "I didn't think detective agencies investigated property taxes."

"Well, of course we do," Mildred said. "Someone has done something with your property taxes, whether it's the state misfiling them or ... something ... and that's where we come in."

"Solving the unsolvable," Aunt Tilde said cheerfully.

Ruth blinked and began to look worried again. "You think finding out what happened to my property taxes is unsolvable?"

"No, of course not," Aunt Tilde said, patting her hand. "That's just our motto, remember? Pretty catchy, isn't it?"

I closed my eyes again and started rubbing my temples, trying to keep away the headache that was threatening to take over.

"Yes, it is catchy," Ruth said, her voice sounding a little stronger, although she still didn't look well.

"So you don't have to worry about a thing," Aunt Tilde said. "We're going to take good care of you."

"Thank you. But ..." Ruth hesitated, the line between her brows deepening. "How much is it going to cost? I don't have much, but whatever I can scrape together is yours."

"Nonsense," Aunt Tilde said cheerfully. "You're a friend. Which means we won't charge you a thing."

Of course we wouldn't. Just because we were supposedly a business didn't mean we needed paying clients. I tried to keep myself from sighing and failed miserably. Aunt Tilde shot me a dirty look.

Ruth looked uncomfortable. "You know, I don't want you to think I'm ungrateful or anything. I do need help to get to the bottom of this property tax kerfuffle. But I also need your help finding Hank, so …" her voice trailed off, and she started plucking at her pants again. "Would it be too much to ask for your help with both cases?"

"Absolutely, we'll help with both," Aunt Tilde said with a broad grin. I ducked my head, so no one would see the look of despair on my face.

Ruth, however, looked relieved. More relieved than she had been during our entire visit. "I can't tell you how much I appreciate that. And I promise I'll pay you as soon as I can."

"Don't you worry about paying us," Aunt Tilde said. "We're here for whatever you need help with. That's what friends are for."

Ruth let out a deep sigh, as if she had been holding her breath for hours, before a flicker of apprehension crossed her face. "Do you really think you could find Hank for me?"

"Absolutely," Aunt Tilde said. Ruth beamed. Mildred, however, looked slightly ill, like she was getting a headache, too.

I felt her pain.

Just like that, we apparently had two cases: fixing Ruth's property tax fiasco and finding the ghost of her missing husband. And we weren't getting paid for either of them.

This was one of those days when I wondered why I even bothered to get up in the morning.

"I can't believe you promised Ruth we are going to find her husband's ghost," Mildred said the moment we were in the car. For once, Mildred and I were on the same page. "What were you thinking?"

"I had to do something," Aunt Tilde said, clutching the steering wheel tightly as she pulled onto the road, nearly hitting a pickup truck parked on the opposite side. "You saw her. She looked like she was about to keel over."

"Well, at least then, she would know where Hank is," Mildred retorted.

Aunt Tilde shot her an unreadable look. "Now, now. You know Ruth has had a tough time. If she thinks her husband's ghost is still with her, what harm can it do?"

Mildred stared at her in disbelief. "She can hire someone, which in this case, appears to be us, to try to find her husband's ghost. That's the harm."

Aunt Tilde clucked her tongue. "How is that harmful? We certainly can spare a few days helping a friend out."

"Does that mean you're going to be the one to tell her we can't find her husband's ghost?" Mildred asked.

"Um ..." Aunt Tilde stumbled on her words. "Well ..."

"My point exactly," Mildred said. "You just promised a woman we would do the impossible. And she's going to be heartbroken when we can't deliver."

I couldn't believe my ears. Mildred was actually making my case for me. Maybe the impossible sometimes did happen.

"Sometimes, you can be such a Negative Nancy," Aunt Tilde said. "Why are you assuming we won't find Hank?"

"Because he's a ghost," Mildred said, her tone exasperated. "Unless you have some sort of ghost-finding skills I don't know about."

"Well, honestly, how hard can it be?" Aunt Tilde said. "It's just a ghost we're talking about. It's not like it can go far."

"How would you know how far a ghost can travel?" Mildred asked, raising her eyebrows. "Are you now an expert in that, as well?"

"In ghost stories, they never go far," Aunt Tilde said. "They basically hang around the place they die."

"Not in Hank's case," Mildred said.

"Well, then, that's probably what happened," Aunt Tilde said triumphantly. "Hank's ghost returned to the place he died. Ruth just needs to visit him there, and all will be well."

"She's not going to like that," Mildred said.

"She'll adjust."

"And how do you propose we convince her his ghost is really there?"

Aunt Tilde drummed her fingers on the steering wheel. "What if we bring the refrigerator message board there and let Hank leave her a message?"

"What, like 'Hi honey, I'm here'?" Mildred asked.

"Well, not that," Aunt Tilde said. "We would need more H's and I's and E's. But we can figure something out."

"Where are you going?" I finally interrupted. "We just passed the turnoff to the agency."

"That's because we're not going to the agency," Aunt Tilde said.

I started to get a bad feeling. "Then where are we going?" *Please don't let it be where I think you're going.*

"You'll see." Aunt Tilde met my eyes in the rearview mirror. "If we're going to save Ruth's house, we'll need the big guns."

Mildred gave her a sharp look. "You'd better not be talking about …"

"That's exactly who I'm talking about," Aunt Tilde said, tightening her grip on the steering wheel, much like my stomach was tightening at the thought of who we were about to see. "We're going to need all the help we can get."

Mildred muttered something under her breath, but she didn't argue. Probably because she knew Aunt Tilde was right.

Just like I knew Aunt Tilde was right, even though I didn't like it, either.

I especially didn't like it when I remembered that I hadn't taken a shower that morning because I had forgotten to set my alarm the night before and had overslept. Therefore, I had simply pulled my plain, brownish-blondish hair back into a ponytail and thrown on an oversized, simple white shirt with khaki shorts that were professional looking enough … but not terribly flattering.

Or how my own makeup was nothing more than a dash of mascara highlighting my blue-gray eyes and a smudge of pink lipstick that, even though I had freshened up before leaving the agency, I was sure was gone now.

For a brief moment, I considered asking Aunt Tilde if she wouldn't mind swinging by the house so I could at least change into something … better, but immediately dismissed it. Not only because Mildred would have a fit if I did that, but also because it shouldn't matter. This was a business meeting, nothing else.

And the sooner I remembered that, the better.

Chapter 7

Stewart and Affiliates had nearly everything a small law office should—a two-room suite in a squat, but well-cared-for, office building. The office for the lawyer was in the back, and in the front was a tiny but neat reception room that barely fit a couch and receptionist desk. It was decorated in a professional (but boring) manner—all beiges and browns. The only thing it lacked was a receptionist. Nick supposedly had one, but I had yet to meet her. I was starting to wonder if she even existed.

The door to Nick's office was mostly closed, but the sound of a male voice drifted out. "Just a minute," the voice called out after a pause.

"This is a mistake," Mildred hissed. "Can't we at least try to see if we can do it ourselves before involving *him*?" She jerked her head toward the office.

"Hush," Aunt Tilde said sternly. "You know we can't. Do you really think we could take on the state of Wisconsin alone?"

"Anything is possible," Mildred said. "You're the one who always says that. Heck, you're the one who thinks we can track down a ghost, so taking on the state of Wisconsin seems like child's play in comparison."

Aunt Tilde made a face. "Finding Hank and convincing the government not to take Ruth's house because she didn't pay her property taxes are two very different issues."

"Maybe that's the problem. We should be combining them instead of separating them," Mildred said. "For instance, maybe we tell the government that Hank was in charge of paying the property tax, and if it wasn't taken care of, they should bring it up with Hank and leave poor Ruth out of it."

"What, you want the state to evict Hank?" Aunt Tilde asked. "You think Ruth will thank us if that's what happens?"

"At least she would be able to stay in her house," Mildred retorted.

"Speaking of Hank," I jumped in before the conversation devolved into what rights Hank had or precisely how the state of Wisconsin was going to evict a ghost. "How did he die?"

Both of their expressions immediately shifted. Aunt Tilde's face fell, whereas Mildred looked enraged. "Oh, it was so sad," Aunt Tilde said. "I felt so terrible for Ruth."

"Death was too good for Hank," Mildred snapped.

I blinked. I wasn't expecting that response. "Um …"

The door flew open. "Sorry about that. Client call."

Nick stood in front of us looking like his typical disheveled self, with his dark-green shirt unbuttoned at the top and his tie loosened around his neck. His black hair was rumpled, like he had been running his fingers through it, and he sported a five o'clock shadow, but his emerald-green eyes were as cool and calculating as ever. As always, my breath seemed to catch in my throat, and I had to scold myself. I had no business feeling this way. He had a girlfriend, and I was dating someone.

I kicked myself again for oversleeping. Maybe I should have asked Aunt Tilde to stop at home after all.

"Well, this is a surprise," he said, eyeing us. His gaze lingered on me for a moment, causing my heart to skip around wildly in my chest. I forced myself to take deep breaths as I ignored the tingling sensation in my stomach that always seemed to happen when I was in his presence. Actually, the tingling seemed more intense than usual, although that might be because I hadn't seen him in a couple of weeks.

Mildred stepped in front of me, breaking his gaze and giving him a stern look. "We're only here because we don't have any other choice, so don't let it go to your head."

"I wouldn't dream of it," Nick said, a faint gleam appearing in his eyes.

Aunt Tilde rolled her eyes. "Oh, for heaven's sake, Mildred. Can't you ask for help nicely, just once in your life?"

"That *was* me asking nicely," Mildred grumbled before shooting me a hard look. "How is Trisha?"

Instantly, it was like I had been drenched with cold water. I reminded myself that I didn't care that Nick had a girlfriend, because I had a boyfriend. Although that didn't mean I liked to think about Trisha. Or about her and Nick together. Actually, I just didn't like thinking about her, period.

"She's fine," Nick said. His tone was neutral and his expression unreadable.

"Good to hear," Mildred said before giving me another hard look. "Everyone your age should have someone special in their life, like how Emily has Jerome. Right, Emily?"

"Um … right," I said. Even though Jerome and I had certainly made up since our fight a couple of weeks before, I also didn't particularly want to discuss my love life with Mildred. Or with Nick, for that matter.

Nick cocked his head, his expression still unreadable. "Is this why you stopped by? To give me an update on Emily and Jeremiah?"

"It's Jerome," I said, my voice a little more snappish than usual.

A wicked grin touched his lips. "Oh yes. My mistake."

"Of course not," Aunt Tilde said, rolling her eyes. "We have a case for you. And she really needs your help."

"Well, then, I guess you should come in," Nick said, pushing the door open wider and gesturing with his arm. "Let me just check and make sure I don't have another meeting scheduled."

"Don't you have a receptionist to do that for you?" I asked as I followed Aunt Tilde and Mildred into his office.

Nick yanked at his tie. "Yes, well, she's on vacation."

I gave him a look of disbelief. "She was on vacation the last time we were here."

Nick shot me a dazzling smile. "What can I say? I'm a very generous boss."

"It's probably more likely that your receptionists keep quitting," Mildred said tartly.

Aunt Tilde nudged her shoulder. "Hush. I'm sure Nick is a wonderful boss."

"Thank you, Tilde," Nick said, his eyes brightening in genuine amusement. "On a related note, I'm guessing this new client isn't a paying client. Am I correct?"

"Oh, but Nick, she's going to lose her house," Aunt Tilde said, clasping her hands together. "We can't let that happen."

"No ma'am," Nick said, leaning down to brush a kiss on Aunt Tilde's cheek as she walked past him into his office. Aunt Tilde smirked and squeezed his arm. Something about the exchange made my chest hurt, both in a good way and a bad way, but I shoved the feeling aside. I had more important concerns than my own confusing feelings. Especially since I had no right to even have them. I was very happy with Jerome.

"Not to mention her husband," Mildred said.

Nick's eyebrows went up. "What? Her husband too?"

"Well, not exactly," Aunt Tilde said. "She already lost her husband, but she's worried that if she loses the house, he won't be able to find her again."

Nick blinked at her. "You're going to have to start at the beginning."

"Trust me, it gets even better," I said to Nick quietly as I passed him, trying not to breathe in the scent of his pine soap, musky aftershave, and unique masculinity, and into the disaster of his office. As usual, his desk was just one giant pile of paper. There were towering piles on every flat surface, although the two chairs in front of his desk were empty for the time being. He waved Mildred and Aunt Tilde toward those chairs, then disappeared to drag another one in behind the empty receptionist desk for me before sitting back down behind his desk. I picked my way over to the chair, trying not to look too closely at all the files that were practically screaming for me to organize them. Not that it was my place. That was Trisha's job, not that she looked like someone who would know how to correctly file her grandmother's homemade recipes. Not that I even knew whether her grandmother cooked or not. Oh man, I needed to get it together, this was getting ridiculous. I forced myself to inhale deeply, the air smelling like coffee, leather, and old books.

"So, how can I help?" he asked, shoving one of the towers of papers aside so he could see all of us. Miraculously, it didn't topple over. He fished a yellow legal pad and pen out of the chaos on his desk.

"It's Ruth Jonasburg," Aunt Tilde said.

Nick frowned. "Why does that name sound familiar?"

"About ten years ago, her husband was murdered by a prostitute," Mildred said.

My jaw dropped. "Wait, what?"

Nick tapped his pen on his pad. "Oh, yes. That's right. I remember now."

"Ruth's husband was murdered by a *prostitute?*" I said again.

"I'm sure it was a misunderstanding," Aunt Tilde said.

"What was the misunderstanding?" I asked. "That he was murdered, or that a prostitute was the one who killed him?"

Aunt Tilde's hands fluttered. "I'm sure Hank didn't mean to get himself mixed up in … well, whatever he was mixed up in."

"Especially since it led to him getting murdered," Mildred said. "Maybe he should have just paid up instead of screwing anyone. At least, not with money."

"Wait, hold on a minute." I held up a hand, still unable to get my head around what Mildred was saying while also trying to square it with the loyal woman sitting in an empty house waiting for her husband's ghost to return. "Hank was with a … prostitute?"

Mildred gave me an exasperated look. "Obviously. Why else would she kill him? Because he was late with his car payment?"

"It might not have been because he was … with a prostitute," Aunt Tilde said, giving both Nick and me a side glance. "There could have been some other reason."

"Like what? He forgot to bring her coffee?"

Aunt Tilde wrinkled her nose. "He was an accountant, not a barista."

Mildred flapped her hands. "Well, maybe Hank screwed up the prostitute's taxes then."

Aunt Tilde pointed at her. "That's what I'm saying. See, that would be a perfect reason for a prostitute to kill Hank. You think a prostitute wants to be audited? That would put a crimp in her business."

Nick furrowed his brow. "You think the prostitute was paying taxes?"

"Of course not," Aunt Tilde said. "I'm sure Hank was hired so the prostitute wouldn't have to pay any taxes. That's the problem."

"Hold on," I said, still trying to get my head around the entire conversation. "Can we go back to Ruth? Does she know that a prostitute killed her husband?"

"Yeah, and I thought you said she was going to lose her husband if she lost the house, but that happened a decade ago," Nick said.

"She lost her husband's physical body a decade ago," Aunt Tilde corrected. "Although, I guess she didn't lose it. It's buried in the Redemption Cemetery."

"Next to one of those gargoyles that move around during Halloween," Mildred said. "At least that's what Ruth told me. They make things very difficult for her."

"Yes, she has trouble finding Hank's grave when they're not where they're supposed to be," Aunt Tilde said. "One time she walked around the graveyard five times before she found Hank."

"There are gargoyles that move?" I asked, feeling more and more bewildered by the conversation. "Aren't gargoyles statues?"

"Normally, yes," Aunt Tilde said. "But you know, it's Redemption, so nothing is what it seems."

"But ... you're talking about statues that *move*," I said. "Statues can't move."

"Well, these can't either, except around Halloween," Aunt Tilde said. "They stay put the rest of the time."

I pressed my fingers against my temples. First ghosts, and now gargoyles. I was definitely getting a headache.

"A lot of people don't believe the gargoyles actually move," Nick said to me. "It's kind of a Redemption urban legend."

"Yes, along with Fire Cottage and Locky," Aunt Tilde said cheerfully.

"Locky?" I stared at Aunt Tilde. "There's something here named Locky?"

"It's our version of the Loch Ness Monster," Aunt Tilde explained. "He lives in Angel Lake."

Seriously? A Loch Ness Monster? And *Fire Cottage*? I wasn't even going to ask. "How many Redemption urban legends are there?"

"Oh, I don't know. Quite a few," Aunt Tilde said.

"It also depends on whether or not you count all the silly ghosts we apparently have flitting around everywhere," Mildred said. "If you include those, there're probably hundreds."

"You don't believe in ghosts either?" I asked Mildred, hardly daring to believe my ears. Was it possible we had even more things in common than I had thought?

Mildred sniffed. "It depends on the ghost. Not all of them are real." She gave Aunt Tilde a hard look.

Aunt Tilde, for her part, looked slightly put-out. "Hank is real. Probably."

"Wait, what do you mean Hank is real?" Nick asked. "Are you saying Hank is a ghost?"

"Well, obviously," Aunt Tilde said. "As you pointed out, he's been dead for a decade. So either he's a ghost or a zombie. I, for one, prefer ghosts. Zombies smell something awful."

"The zombie might be more helpful around the house though," Mildred said. "I bet he would have done a better job with the yard than Bradley did."

"A zombie certainly couldn't have done a worse job," I muttered.

"Who's Bradley?" Nick asked.

"The con artist," Aunt Tilde said. "He's the reason why Ruth is going to lose her house."

"Because he did a bad job with her yard?" Nick asked.

"No, because he stole her property taxes," Mildred said.

"How does a gardener steal someone's property taxes?" Nick asked.

"When you hire a gardener to do your accounting, that's how," Mildred said.

"Technically, she didn't hire him, as she never paid him," Aunt Tilde said.

Mildred flapped her hands. "What do you mean she didn't pay him? He stole her property taxes!"

"Yes, but I'm sure Ruth wouldn't have agreed to pay Bradley her property taxes in exchange for helping her with her accounting," Aunt Tilde said before frowning. "Pretty sure, at least."

"Why would Ruth hire a gardener to do her accounting?" Nick asked.

"I just explained she didn't hire Bradley ..." Aunt Tilde began.

"I meant," Nick interrupted, flashing Aunt Tilde a quick, devastating smile. "Why was Ruth having a gardener help her with her accounting?"

"Probably because he was so dreadful at gardening, she assumed he would do better with accounting," Mildred said.

"In her defense, Hank was no help either," Aunt Tilde said.

Nick gave her a confused look. "Hank ... the ghost?"

"Unfortunately for Ruth, Hank the zombie probably wouldn't have been any better either," Mildred said. "At least not with the accounting. I still say he would have been a far better gardener."

Nick pinched the bridge of his nose as he squeezed his eyes tightly for a moment. "Maybe you'd better start at the beginning. What exactly does Ruth need help with?"

Aunt Tilde held up one finger. "Finding Hank." She held up a second finger. "Keeping the government from taking her house."

Nick looked alarmed. "Someone stole Hank's body? We have a grave robber in Redemption?" Another thought occurred to him then, and he looked even more alarmed. "Wait. Was it Halloween? Were the gargoyles moving, and she couldn't find Hank's grave?"

"I think the gargoyles are still where they're supposed to be," Aunt Tilde said. "Although I will admit, I haven't checked on them lately."

"Maybe one of the gargoyles can move in with Ruth if Hank doesn't come back," Mildred said.

Nick stared at her. "Hold on. Is *Ruth t*he grave robber? Did she steal Hank's body, and now it's gone missing?"

"I don't think Ruth has the strength to dig up a grave," Mildred said. "She would have needed Bradley's help to do that."

"No, no, no, he just stole her property taxes," Aunt Tilde said. "I'm sure Bradley wasn't digging up any bodies. After all, he was a terrible gardener, so I doubt he enjoys digging in the dirt."

"Hank's body isn't what's missing," I broke in. At this rate, the government would seize Ruth's house before Nick even understood what the problem was.

"Although to be fair, we don't know that for sure," Aunt Tilde said. "Maybe we should swing by the cemetery, just to be on the safe side."

I shot Aunt Tilde a look. "I have no doubt Hank's body is exactly where it's supposed to be. What is missing, at least according to Ruth, is Hank the ghost."

For a long moment, Nick simply stared at me. "I'm sorry," he said finally. "I thought you said that Hank the ghost is missing."

"That's exactly what she said," Mildred said with a sigh.

"But ... how does a ghost even go missing?" Nick asked.

"Same as the living do. Go out for cigarettes and don't come back," Mildred said.

Nick blinked. "The ghost went out for ... cigarettes?"

"No, of course not," Aunt Tilde said. "Hank doesn't smoke."

"Not that you know of," Mildred said.

"I don't understand. How do you know if a ghost has gone missing? For that matter, how do you even know if you have a ghost?" Nick asked.

It took a bit of back and forth, but eventually, Aunt Tilde and Mildred filled Nick in on how Hank the ghost apparently went missing, although Mildred made it clear she didn't believe there even was a Hank the ghost.

"You should keep an open mind," Aunt Tilde said to Mildred.

"And you expect me to believe that YOU believe in Hank the ghost?" Mildred asked.

"If it makes Ruth happy, I believe it," Aunt Tilde said firmly before a sadness swept over her face. "Besides, it's probably partly my fault that Ruth thinks there is a ghost. If I had made more time for her ... if she hadn't been so lonely, maybe she wouldn't feel the need to bring back her husband's ghost."

"Tilde, this is absolutely *not* your fault," Mildred said firmly.

"I agree," Nick said. "Ruth is a grown woman and can make her own choices, which you are not responsible for."

"I agree as well," I said. "There's no way this is your fault."

"Besides, you have the kindest heart of anyone I know," Nick continued. "If anything, it's the system's fault for allowing it to get so far with her property-tax issue. Maybe someone should have picked up the phone to see what was going on."

"Exactly," Mildred said with a sniff. "We certainly pay enough in taxes. You would think we could get something for our money. Or maybe Lynne should have seen something and stepped in. Something definitely went sideways here, but it has nothing to do with you."

Aunt Tilde took a deep breath and gave us all a watery smile. "Thank you all. I appreciate what you're saying. And while I agree that others certainly share the blame, this is why we must help her." She paused, her eyes sharp and clear behind her orange-rimmed glasses as she looked at each of us. "Don't you see? This is why we must save her house. Not just because it's the right thing to do, but because if we don't, I don't know what will happen. She'll believe she's leaving Hank behind, and he won't be able to find her, and … well, I don't know if she will recover."

There was a long moment of silence as Aunt Tilde's words sank in. Even though she hadn't said it outright, I knew what she meant.

And, picturing how sad and lost Ruth looked every time she talked about her husband being gone, I didn't think she was wrong.

"Well, then, we'd better get started," Nick said briskly.

Chapter 8

"Let's start at the beginning," Nick said, his pen poised on note-book. "How exactly did Bradley steal Ruth's property taxes to begin with?"

I quickly jumped in to summarize the important details before Aunt Tilde and Mildred could sidetrack the conversation again. As I talked, Nick took notes while both Mildred and Aunt Tilde tried to elbow their way into the conversation.

"So, what are you thinking?" Nick asked when I was more or less finished. "That Bradley stole the checks meant for the government and cashed them himself?"

"Maybe at first," I said. "And once she gave him access to her checking account, I'm guessing he just wrote checks to himself."

Nick frowned. "I can't believe he would be *that* sloppy."

"That's what happens when you hire a gardener to do your ac-counting," Mildred said.

"Yes, but what if Ruth noticed? How would he explain it? I'm sure she must have at least glanced at her bank statements, right?" Nick asked, looking between Aunt Tilde and Mildred.

There was a long, awkward pause. Aunt Tilde was careful to fo-cus her gaze on Nick as Mildred sighed and shook her head.

Nick put his pen down and rubbed between his eyes.

"It's not her fault," Aunt Tilde said defensively. "You know how Hank was. He took care of all the finances for her. She's never had to deal with any of that before."

"Which is why it's such a surprise that Hank—the ghost—didn't do anything to help her out," Mildred said sarcastically, rolling her eyes.

"That doesn't mean he wasn't real," Aunt Tilde said.

"I think it's a pretty good indication he wasn't real," Mildred said. "He was her husband, after all. If anyone would realize how much help Ruth would need, it would be him. I would think the first thing Hank's ghost would do would be to teach her how to balance her checkbook."

"How? By flickering the lights on and off? Spelling words on the fridge?" Aunt Tilde asked.

"How does a ghost spell words on a fridge?" Nick wondered.

"Not easily," Aunt Tilde said. "Especially since there's only one of each letter. Talk about wanting to pull your hair out. Assuming a ghost even has hair."

"Anyway," I said, trying to pull the conversation back. "What do you suggest we do to help?"

"Well, the first thing we need to do is to figure out what exactly Bradley did," Nick said. "The only thing we know for sure is the property taxes haven't been paid, and Bradley was supposedly the one in charge of making sure they were. But what exactly happened? Did he actually steal the money?"

"Of course he did," Mildred said. "Where else did the money go if not into his pocket?"

Nick gave her a hard look. "Are you sure? All I heard was that he offered to drop the checks in the mail for her."

"I'm pretty sure she said the checks were cashed," I said. "At least I thought she did."

"So, if she knows the checks were cashed, then she would probably have noticed if Bradley is writing checks to himself, right?" Nick said.

"In theory," I said, remembering Ruth's confusion.

"This is why we need to start by getting to the bottom of what exactly happened," Nick said. "At a minimum, we need to do an audit of her books. That will help us determine whether Bradley committed a crime, or if he was just negligent. I'll also need to see her correspondence with the state of Wisconsin, as much as she has. We probably should set up a meeting. Do you think Ruth would be willing to talk to me?"

"Of course she would," Aunt Tilde said.

"Even though she probably shouldn't," Mildred said, giving Nick a hard look. "She's way too trusting. That's why she's in this predicament."

"Do you want my help or not?" Nick asked.

Mildred made a face. "Fine." She sounded put out, like it was Nick who was asking for help.

"Is there anyone else we can talk to?" Nick asked. "Maybe a neighbor? Someone else who may have met this elusive Bradley?"

"There's Lynne," Aunt Tilde said. "She lives across the street and often stops by to help Ruth. If anyone could help, it would be her."

"We stopped by to talk to her, but she wasn't home," I said. For some irrational reason, I wanted Nick to know we weren't completely clueless about how to run a proper investigation. No, we hadn't asked Ruth for the proper paperwork before we left her, but that was because I had assumed we would be back with a list of questions and items to get. I didn't realize, although I probably should have, that Aunt Tilde was going to bring Nick into this case. A part of me really wanted to explain all of that, even as I told myself it didn't matter what Nick thought. He was simply someone who could provide Ruth with expertise we didn't have. That was all.

Nick glanced up from his notes and gave me a small, knowing smile—as if he could hear my mental argument. I gritted my teeth. Ugh. From that point on, I needed to bring my own car to client meetings. Then, I wouldn't be held hostage to Aunt Tilde's whims.

Not to mention, at the very least, I could stop somewhere and freshen up my makeup.

"Also, we didn't take the notice from the state, but I did write down the pertinent information," I said crisply, pulling my notebook out of my bag. I flipped it to the right page and handed it to Nick. "It didn't feel right taking her correspondence, but I wanted to have as much information as possible. I'm sure we can get the original when we audit her bank accounts."

Nick's smug smile seemed to widen as he accepted my notebook and glanced at the page. "Nice penmanship," he said, giving me a sly look. "Very professional."

I crossed my legs and glared at him.

"Emily does have very nice penmanship," Aunt Tilde said warmly, giving me a genuine, proud-aunty smile. "Even as a little girl, she had beautiful handwriting. She even won an award for it. Emily, was it fourth grade? Or maybe it was seventh?"

"Fifth," I said through clenched teeth, trying to ignore the gleam in Nick's dark-green eyes. I didn't mention I had also won in sixth grade, as well.

"Good penmanship is so important," Mildred said, sitting up straighter. "In fact, according to scientists, there's a link between it and intelligence. I have to say that I've found that to be true with my own students." She gave Nick an icy look, and his smirk dimmed. "The messier the handwriting, the more chaotic the thinking. That's what I always say."

"Then why do doctors have such bad handwriting?" Aunt Tilde asked.

"Because they don't," Mildred said, shaking her head in disgust. "I can't believe you fell for it."

"Fell for what?" Aunt Tilde asked. "Doctors having bad handwriting? But they do. You've seen Dr. Benson's handwriting. It's barely legible."

Mildred waved her hand. "It's all fake. They're just pretending to have bad handwriting."

"Why would they do that?" I asked. Not that I thought there was any link between good penmanship and intelligence (even though I did have excellent handwriting), but pretending to have bad handwriting made no sense.

"Because it makes them more relatable," Mildred said. "If you realized how smart they were, you might not listen to them. No one wants to be told what to do by a smarty-pants." She glanced at me. "Not you, Emily. You're much too sweet to be one. Not like those over-educated doctors." She sniffed.

"But don't you want your doctor to be smarter than you?" I asked, deciding it was safer to concentrate on doctors rather than try to figure out if and how I was being insulted.

"Of course," Mildred said, her voice surprised. "But you don't want them to rub it in your face. No one likes that."

"Um … I guess not," I said.

"Well, with that logic, maybe lawyers are also pretending to have bad handwriting," Nick said, giving me a quick wink. "You know, so their clients will be more likely to listen to them."

Mildred narrowed her eyes and lowered her chin, so she was looking down at Nick. "Don't you try to play those games with me, young man. I saw your handwriting before you got yourself all those fancy degrees. I know *exactly* how your penmanship links to your intelligence."

"Oh, Mildred, you're too hard on the boy," Aunt Tilde said as Nick ducked his head, a sheepish expression on his face. "Nick is a good boy, and he did very well in his education ... even if you can't read a word he writes."

"So, back to the tax situation," I said, wanting to get the conversation back on track. We were there to help Ruth, after all, not to discuss who had the best penmanship. But I would be lying if I also didn't feel just a tiny bit bad for Nick. It was hard not to when Mildred flipped into teacher mode. I often found myself feeling sorry for all her students who had ever been on the receiving end of her ire. "We should set up a meeting between you and Ruth as soon as possible, and as part of that meeting, you're going to want to do an audit, correct? Is there anything else we should be doing?"

"Other than figuring out what Bradley's last name is, I can't think of anything," Nick said. He flashed me a quick grin as if he knew I was trying to distract Mildred, and I could feel the warmth of that smile travel throughout my body. I quickly looked away, telling myself to stop that nonsense. I was there to do a job, not whatever was happening to my physical body. Worse, if I didn't get my head into the game, the person who would suffer most was Ruth.

Mildred snorted. "For all we know, Bradley isn't even his real name. Besides, according to Ruth, she hasn't seen him for months. He's probably lying on the beach somewhere enjoying his ill-gotten gains."

"I seriously doubt he's on a beach," Aunt Tilde scoffed. "There's no way he made enough money off of Ruth to have retired. He's probably scamming his next gardening client."

"Hopefully, others would be a little more discerning about hiring a gardener to do their accounting," Mildred said, shaking her head sadly. "As much as I love Ruth, she's always been a little too trusting for her own good."

"I know," Aunt Tilde said, letting out a deep sigh. "That's why Hank was so good for her. She probably should have let Hank keep doing the books."

"Hank … the ghost?" Nick asked.

"Who else?" Aunt Tilde said. "Even as a ghost, he couldn't have done a worse job than Bradley. At the very least, he wouldn't have any reason to scam Ruth. It's not like ghosts need money."

"Other than for cigarettes," Mildred said.

"Hold on," I said as a thought occurred to me. "Didn't Ruth say that Bradley knew Hank from work?"

Mildred shot me an exasperated look. "Oh, for goodness' sake. Emily, you don't believe that, do you? Clearly, he was lying."

"Well, maybe he was," I said. "But isn't it at least worth looking into? There had to be a reason why Bradley targeted her, and maybe he really did work with Hank at some point."

There was an awkward pause as Nick, Mildred, and Aunt Tilde exchanged a look.

"What?" I demanded. "Why is that so strange? If nothing else, it would at least give us a place to start looking. Someone has to know this guy. Redemption isn't that big of a town."

Aunt Tilde cleared her throat. "It's not that. I just think it would be a waste of time."

"Why?" I asked. "Is the place where he used to work no longer in business?"

"No, it's still there," Mildred said. "It's one of the largest employers in town. Redemption Manufacturing."

"Then why shouldn't we investigate that connection?" I asked again. "Unless … does it have something to do with how Hank died? Speaking of which, what IS the story?"

"It was so awful," Aunt Tilde said. "Such a tragedy."

"For Ruth," Mildred said, folding her arms across her chest. "Hank, on the other hand, deserved everything he got."

"You keep saying that," I said. "But what exactly happened? How do you know a prostitute killed Hank?"

"We don't," Aunt Tilde said, shooting a hard look at Mildred. "We don't know what happened. No one does."

"Yes, because there's a perfectly innocent explanation for Hank being found in a back alley where all the prostitutes hang out," Mildred said, her words dripping with sarcasm.

"Maybe he took a wrong turn," Aunt Tilde said. "It happens. You're not paying attention to where you're going, and the next thing you know, you find yourself behind a dumpster."

"With your pants down?" Mildred asked incredulously.

"His belt probably broke," Aunt Tilde said. "Ruth told me she had meant to buy him a new belt but hadn't gotten around to it."

"Yes, I'm sure it was the belt, and the prostitutes had nothing to do with it," Mildred said.

"Even if prostitutes were in the alley, it doesn't necessarily mean Hank was cheating," Aunt Tilde said.

"What else were they doing back there?" Mildred asked, raising an eyebrow. "Playing cards?"

"Maybe they were," Aunt Tilde said.

Mildred looked at her in exasperation. "Yes, because Hank always plays cards with his pants down."

"They could have been playing strip poker," Aunt Tilde said.

"Then what happened to the cards?" Mildred asked.

"They probably took them with them," Aunt Tilde said. "Why would anyone leave a perfectly good pack of cards in an alley? Besides, they could have had another game they had to get to."

"Yes, you're right. Those weren't hookers hanging in the back alley. They were card sharks," Mildred said sarcastically.

Aunt Tilde flapped her hands at Mildred. "You don't know anything more than I do about what happened in that alley. It very well could have been a big misunderstanding."

"Yes, it definitely was," Mildred said, rolling her eyes. "Hank just tripped and found his you-know-what inside-"

"Tilde has a point," Nick quickly interrupted, rubbing the back of his neck. "The entire case was circumstantial. While it's true Hank was found in a rather ... compromising position, the cops weren't able to find enough evidence to arrest anyone."

"So, it's still unsolved?" I asked.

"Which is part of the problem," Aunt Tilde said. "Ruth insists there's a reasonable explanation for all of that ... unpleasantness ..."

Mildred rolled her eyes again at that, "but rather than do their job, the cops only wanted to focus on the most titillating aspect of the case."

"Probably because it was the only thing that made sense," Mildred said.

Nick tapped his pen against his notebook. "Not necessarily. It's possible it was just a robbery gone wrong."

"Then why was he there in the first place?" Mildred asked.

"And that's the problem," Aunt Tilde said. "Everyone assumes they know what happened. And you know what happens when people assume, right?"

"What?" I asked.

"They make an ass out of you and me," Aunt Tilde said decisively.

Mildred rolled her eyes again. "If it walks like a duck and quacks like a duck, it's probably a duck."

"It's true that it didn't look … great for Hank," Nick broke in. "Nor did it help when the prostitute went missing, along with all that money."

"Wait, a prostitute went missing, too?" My head was starting to spin. "And how much money are we talking about?"

"Quack, quack," Mildred said.

Nick pressed his lips together before turning back to me. "There was a young prostitute, early twenties or so. A couple of Hank's co-workers claimed they saw him with her …"

"Quack," Mildred said again.

"They saw him buy her a sandwich once," Aunt Tilde said, glaring at Mildred.

Mildred opened her mouth, but Nick held up a hand. "We know what it looks like, Mildred. But again, Tilde is right. There could be an innocent explanation."

"I'm so confused," I said. "He bought a prostitute a sandwich, and then she disappeared with his money?"

"You forgot to mention what else he bought her," Mildred said darkly.

"Oh, for heaven's sake," Aunt Tilde said. "Get your mind out of the gutter."

Mildred opened her mouth to respond, but Nick quickly cut her off. "Maybe we should start at the beginning. Hank was found dead in an alley. He had been stabbed in the chest with a little pocket-knife, which was small enough that, under normal circumstances, it likely wouldn't have been enough to kill a grown man. But as luck would have it, it punctured the main artery next to his heart. The coroner thought he had bled out in minutes. As Mildred so color-fully pointed out," Mildred smirked at that, "his pants were around his ankles. Plus, he had been robbed. The police assumed Hank had solicited a prostitute, but something had gone wrong with the trans-action, and she killed him and took off with the money."

"I'll tell you what went wrong with the *transaction*," Mildred said. "He refused to pay her. That's what went wrong."

"Hank wouldn't do that," Aunt Tilde said.

"Which part?" I asked. "Hire a hooker or not pay her?"

"Either," Aunt Tilde said firmly.

"How would you know?" Mildred asked. "Did he ever solicit you for sex?"

"Oh please," Aunt Tilde said, shaking her head. "He couldn't af-ford me."

I nearly choked at that.

"Anyway," Nick said, choking a little himself. "During the inves-tigation, it came out that Hank had been seen in that area, mostly near a bar called the Lone Man Standing, although it's not there anymore."

"What happened to it?" I asked.

"It burned down," Mildred said, pursing her lips. "Under very suspicious circumstances." She eyed Aunt Tilde, who frowned at her.

"Oh, you can't think Hank had anything to do with it. He was long dead by the time it burned down."

"Well, his ghost is apparently still hanging around, so who knows what's going on," Mildred said.

"Anyway," Nick continued. "That's never been a great area of Re-demption. There's a new bar there now, The Jack Saloon, and it still has just as many problems as the Lone Man Standing. Regardless, Hank was apparently seen there, and while it's possible he was just stopping by for a quick drink after work, it's not exactly known as the sort of place accountants stop for a drink after work, so of course, that only fueled all the rumors. Then, when it came out that Hank had been seen buying a sandwich for one of the prostitutes a few days before he died, and that prostitute had gone missing, well ..." he lifted his hands helplessly.

"As I said before, quack, quack," Mildred said smugly.

I was starting to agree with Mildred.

"While it's true it looks bad," Aunt Tilde said. "There's still no evidence that's what happened."

"What are you talking about, no evidence?" Mildred asked. "How much evidence do you need?"

"We don't know why he was there," Aunt Tilde said. "Ruth always said Hank worked a lot ..."

"Oh, yeah, he was working alright," Mildred said.

Aunt Tilde ignored her. "One of his coworkers also said he had been really excited that day—that he had planned some big celebration for Ruth. He wouldn't tell anyone what it was. Would he really be doing that if he were paying prostitutes?"

"Do you really want an answer to that?" Mildred asked.

Aunt Tilde glared at her. "I'm just saying, it might not be what it seems. You met Hank. Did he ever strike you as someone who would cheat on his wife?"

"Absolutely," Mildred said. "I knew there was something off with him the moment I laid eyes on him."

Aunt Tilde narrowed her eyes. "You said no such thing. In fact, I think your exact words were that he was 'as bland as toast.'"

"Just because he was bland doesn't mean he wasn't cheating on her," Mildred said.

"He worshipped Ruth," Aunt Tilde said. "You could see it in the way he treated her. He would never cheat on her."

"Then how do you explain him ending up in an alley?" Mildred asked.

Aunt Tilde's shoulders slumped. "I don't know." She sounded pained to admit it. "That's the problem. But there has to be another explanation. There just has to be. Ruth ..." Her voice trailed off as she squeezed her eyes shut and shook her head.

Nick let out a sigh and rubbed the bridge of his nose. "I know. What happened to Ruth was awful, especially since it wasn't even her fault. But at this point, I don't think there's much we can do. I'm not saying there isn't another explanation. But after all this time, I'm not sure we'd be able to find it. We might be able to right one wrong, at least, by keeping the state from foreclosing on her home. I know it's not going to fix everything, but it's one thing, and sometimes, one thing is all you need."

"Plus, if she keeps her house, Hank the ghost might come back, as well, and then we would have solved both her problems," Mildred said.

"Oh, that's right. We have to find Hank, as well," Aunt Tilde said before cutting her eyes toward me. "Emily, can you make a note? We need to start researching all the various ways to find a ghost."

Seriously? Although this was Aunt Tilde we were talking about. Why would I think she wouldn't be serious?

Aunt Tilde was watching me, her expression expectant, so with a hard swallow (and a sinking heart) I wrote in my notebook, "Research ways to find a ghost."

Please, please, please let that not end up on my to-do list.

Nick made a slight face as he started shuffling the papers on his desk. "Tell you what. I'll focus on the property tax issue while you look for Hank. Deal?"

Aunt Tilde perked up, even as Mildred looked to have just swallowed a fly. I could commiserate, as I was feeling the same way.

"Deal," Aunt Tilde said cheerfully.

Chapter 9

"Emily, got a second?" Nick asked casually. Almost too casually.

The three of us had just gotten up to leave, as we had our marching orders, even if we didn't particularly care for them. (Although, maybe that was just me. And perhaps Mildred. Aunt Tilde looked thrilled.)

Mildred answered for me. "Sure, what else do you need?"

Nick had stood up as well, and he stuffed his hands into the pockets of his light-brown pants. "Just a moment with Emily."

Mildred folded her arms across her chest. "Whatever you need to say to Emily, you can say in front of all of us."

I touched Mildred's shoulder. "It's fine. Why don't you and Aunt Tilde go out into the lobby and give Ruth a call? The sooner we can get that audit done, the better."

Mildred narrowed her eyes suspiciously as her head swiveled between me and Nick. I could see she was torn. On the one hand, she knew I was right; the faster we moved on the property tax mess, the more likely we were to stop the foreclosure. But she also didn't trust Nick, as she was convinced he was going to break my heart. Fat chance of that, seeing how we weren't even dating. Heck, I wasn't even sure we were friends. Not to mention he had a girlfriend.

"We also could just drive over and talk to Ruth in person, as well," Aunt Tilde piped in.

Mildred whirled around to face Aunt Tilde. "What? We can't leave Emily here. How will she get home?"

"We can swing back around and pick her up when we're done," Aunt Tilde said.

"That, or I can give her a ride," Nick said.

Mildred turned back to glare at him. "Don't you have work to do?"

"Nothing that can't wait for the time it takes for me to drive her back to the agency." Nick's voice was mild, and his face was expressionless, but I could see the gleam in his eyes.

"Honestly, I'll be fine," I said. "Go call Ruth, and by the time you're off the phone, I'm sure I'll be done."

Mildred pressed her lips together into a flat line. "Fine. But don't think this means I won't be paying attention."

Nick nodded solemnly. "I would expect nothing less."

Mildred gave him another sharp look, as if trying to decide if he was making fun of her, but Nick's expression was suitably meek enough that she finally followed Aunt Tilde into the lobby area. Aunt Tilde shut the door firmly behind her, but not before I heard another squabble about keeping the door open.

"Mildred, for heaven's sake. They're both adults, not two teenagers making out in one of their bedrooms." Aunt Tilde's voice floated through the door, and I could immediately feel my cheeks redden even as I bit my lip to keep from laughing.

I looked at Nick, who appeared to be doing the same. "For the record, I never brought a girl home when I was a teenager."

I stared at him in disbelief. "I don't believe for a second that you never … did anything with a girl when you were a teenager." My mouth had dried out, and I found myself unable to say the words "made out," or even worse, "kissed."

His smile turned lethal. "Who said I never 'did anything' with a girl? If that was my goal, there were plenty of places in Redemption I could take someone for some … privacy."

Oh man. My face was so hot, it felt like it was on fire. Even worse, the way he was grinning at me, he knew how embarrassed I was.

I took a step back. "Is this what you wanted to speak to me about, or is there something else I can help you with?"

As soon as the words were out of my mouth, I wanted to snatch them back. Nick, on the other hand, couldn't have looked more entertained than if I had whipped out three swords and started juggling them.

"If you put it like that, there's a lot I could use your … *help* with, but I suspect Mildred isn't going to give us that kind of time." He flashed another grin at me. The way the conversation was going, I was sure I was going to look like I'd gotten a terrible sunburn. "You're cute when you blush, you know."

I rolled my eyes in an effort to keep myself from turning even more red. "I'm leaving."

He held up his hands. "Okay, okay. I just wanted to give you a … heads up, I guess, about Ruth."

I frowned. This was the last thing I expected him to say, and I couldn't decide if I was relieved or disappointed. "Ruth? What do you mean?"

He sighed, running his hand through his hair. "Look," he said, lowering his voice as he glanced at the door. "Obviously, there's still a lot we don't know, but it sure sounds like this Bradley person stole the money that should have been used for her property taxes, which means she won't have it. If that's the case, I can certainly try talking to the state to see if we can get some sort of extension, but if they're already moving toward foreclosure … well, it may not work. And if Ruth thinks she has to stay there because her husband's ghost is going to return, but she can't, because the state forecloses on it …" His voice trailed off.

"You think she's going to have a breakdown?" I guessed. "Or maybe refuse to leave?"

He lifted his palms into the air. "I have no idea what she'll do. I doubt *she* knows what she'll do. But I think it would be smart to start making plans to deal with the worst-case scenario."

I blinked. "Me? But I have no idea what needs to be done."

He smiled at me, a genuine one, not like the cocky grin he had been flashing before. "If anyone can figure it out, it's you."

"Yes, but …" I was flustered again, but it was for a completely different reason than earlier. It wasn't just his words, but that smile … I couldn't even think straight. *Enough Emily*, I told myself sternly. *Remember, he has a girlfriend.* That helped, as it was equivalent to getting drenched with cold water. "I'm not even sure where to start."

He shifted his weight from one foot to the other. "Yeah, that's why I wanted to tell you now. This whole thing could go sideways in a hurry. I don't know if there's anything you can do to track down Hank's ghost, but that might be a good place to start."

"Oh geez." Great. Now I was going to have no choice but to get sucked into investigating a missing ghost. Was it even possible to find a ghost? This was turning into a nightmare. "I guess I'll need to bone up on my paranormal hunting."

The corner of his mouth twitched up. "Maybe that can turn into another service The Redemption Detective Agency offers."

"What? No, don't you dare mention anything to Aunt Tilde." It was all I could do to not clap my hand over his mouth just in case she happened to be standing by the closed door. I couldn't even imagine what a disaster that would be. All the ghost-hunting equipment Mildred would want to buy … Nora bringing cookies and Smoke, her crazy cat, into some supposedly haunted place where who knew what would happen.

Ugh.

"I wouldn't dream of it," Nick said solemnly, although his eyes were laughing at me. I glared at him. Of course he would find it funny. He wasn't the one who was going to have to figure out how to talk some disgruntled homeowner out of suing us because Smoke peed on their couch.

"But speaking of Tilde …" he paused, as if trying to arrange the words in his head. "You may also want to keep an eye on her. She already feels guilty enough about Ruth, and if the worst does happen to her, I could see Tilde taking it really hard."

Oh man. Nick was right. Aunt Tilde would be nearly as devastated as Ruth if everything went to pieces. Even if I wasn't already motivated enough to try to help Ruth as much as I could, this thought added even more urgency to the issue.

"I'll keep an eye on her," I said.

Nick nodded, his eyes never leaving mine. "I know you will."

Our gazes locked. For a moment, we just stared at each other, and even though I knew it was a ridiculous notion, as we weren't suited for each other at all (as exemplified even by the state of his office, for heaven's sake), I found myself wishing things could be different. That we weren't dating other people.

But that was silly. Not only were we incompatible, but he was a lawyer—and I had sworn all lawyers off after my former lawyer-fiancé dumped me.

Nevertheless, I couldn't tear my eyes away from him.

He sucked in his breath. "Emily, I …"

Crash.

Both of us jumped as if we had been caught doing something we shouldn't have been, even though we weren't even touching.

"What the …" he said, as we both turned toward the door. It had come from Nick's reception area, where Aunt Tilde and Mildred were supposedly calling Ruth while they waited for me.

"I'd better see what just happened," I said, moving toward the door, my thoughts a tangled mess. I told myself it was good that we were interrupted, even if it didn't feel that way at the moment.

But before I could reach the door, it flew open, and Trisha stalked in with Mildred and Aunt Tilde hot on her heels.

"There you are," Trisha said, like she had been searching all over for Nick only to find him in his office. As usual, she was perfectly put together with a silky dark-blue blouse, black pencil skirt, and black high heels. Her black hair was pulled up into a bun with a few loose tendrils framing her perfectly made-up face. Again, the image of myself with my messy, unwashed ponytail, no makeup, and pro-fessionally adequate but hardly flattering outfit flitted through my mind, and I wanted to slink away. Had I really been contemplating dating Nick? Why would he even give me a second look with her on his arm? Ugh.

Trisha, as usual, was completely oblivious of me. "Why did you hire those two to be your new receptionists?"

Nick stared at her. "What?"

Mildred straightened her spine, an offended expression on her face. "I am NOT a receptionist."

Trisha rolled her eyes. "Personal assistant, then. Whatever."

I didn't think it was possible, but Mildred looked even more of-fended. "How dare you. I don't work for Nick."

"Well, then why are you here bothering the real receptionist?" Trisha asked before leaning in closer to Nick. In a loud whisper, asked, "And why would you hire her? The other one at least dresses decently."

"Wait a minute, are you talking about me? What's wrong with my outfit?" Aunt Tilde looked down at her flowing purple shirt and hot-pink pants as she adjusted her bright-orange glasses.

"You definitely match more than normal," Mildred agreed, smoothing down her pressed, green pantsuit, looking a little more mollified now that Trisha had recognized her good taste in clothes.

Nick, however, looked pained. "Trisha, what are you doing here?"

Trisha let out a tinkling little laugh that reminded me of nails on a chalkboard as she slapped Nick's shoulder. "Oh, you're such a kidder."

"And what was that crash?" I asked, making a point of not looking at the comfortable way Trisha was hanging on Nick.

"Oh, a vase fell over," Mildred said, waving a hand.

"A vase?" I was trying to remember if I had seen a vase when we first walked in, but I couldn't picture it. "What vase?"

"The one in the drawer," Aunt Tilde said, like it should have been obvious.

"A drawer?" I asked. "You mean, the desk drawer?"

"Well, of course," Mildred said, like it should have been obvious. "What other drawer would we be talking about?"

"But why were you going through the desk in the first place?" I asked.

"How else would we have found the vase?" Mildred asked.

"It looks very nice on the desk," Aunt Tilde said. "At least it did. Until it fell off."

"I think one of the legs is loose," Mildred said. "It was really wobbly." She lowered her chin so she could give Nick a hard look above her glasses. "It's quite a safety hazard."

"Yes, the desk does have a bad leg," Nick said. "That's why we put it in the drawer. So it wouldn't fall off and break."

"Oh, the vase will be fine," Aunt Tilde said. "Nothing a little glue can't fix."

Trisha poked Nick. "You really need to get someone in here to help you with hiring."

"Wait … you want me to hire someone to help me with hiring?" Nick asked.

"I keep telling you that you need an office manager," Trisha said, looking around Nick's messy office as she wrinkled her perfect nose. "That would make more sense than a receptionist with ... unusual taste in clothes."

"Why thank you," Aunt Tilde said, preening a little.

Trisha rolled her eyes. "It wasn't a-"

"Tilde, were you able to get in touch with Ruth?" Nick interrupted.

"Yes, she's expecting you tomorrow," Aunt Tilde said.

"We'll be there, as well," Mildred said, narrowing her eyes.

"That's not necessary," Nick said.

"Oh, I think it is," Mildred said.

"But it might make more sense for you to work on another part of the case," Nick said. "Like finding Hank."

"Hank." Mildred shook her head. "Like that's even a thing."

"Nick is right," Aunt Tilde said. "We should be looking for Hank. I'm sure Ruth is very worried right now."

"If that's the case, we should start tonight, so we'll be ready for Nick's meeting with Ruth tomorrow," Mildred said before glancing at me. "Although you don't have to join us, Emily, if you have plans with *Jerome* tonight."

"Um ..." I didn't have plans with Jerome, but I also wasn't all that excited about researching ghost hunting. What I really wanted to do was take Scout for a nice walk before enjoying a quiet meal and a good book.

But before I could figure out how to answer, Trisha's face lit up. "Oh, you're still dating Jerome?"

"Yeeess," I said, unsure where she was going.

"The principal, right?"

"Um, yes," I said again, starting to feel even more uncomfortable. Nick had an unreadable expression on his face, and Mildred took a step closer to me.

"Trisha, however, seemed completely oblivious. "We should go on a double date."

"Wait, what?" I asked.

"What?" Nick echoed.

Trisha turned to Nick. "It would be fun. The four of us."

"Trisha, I don't know …" Nick said. He was looking as uncomfortable as I felt.

"That's a terrible idea," Mildred said flatly.

"Oh, nonsense," Aunt Tilde said. "I think it's a great idea."

Trisha beamed at Aunt Tilde. "See? Your receptionist agrees."

Nick looked pained. "Maybe we should talk about this first."

"Why?" She turned to me. "Don't you think it would be fun?"

"I really should ask Jerome first," I said weakly.

"Oh, I'm sure you'll be able to convince him," Trisha said confidently. "Shall we say later this week? Maybe Thursday night?" She had such an expectant look on her face, I wasn't sure how to refuse.

"Maybe we should let Emily talk to Jeremiah first," Nick said.

"Jerome," I automatically corrected.

"Oh Nick." Trisha rolled her eyes. "You're such a joker. But you better remember his name on Thursday."

"I'll do my best," Nick said.

"I don't think this is a good idea at all," Mildred said, giving me a knowing look. I could almost hear her telling me how I needed to be careful of Trisha, because obviously, she would rather be with Jerome than Nick. I wasn't so sure about that.

"Of course it is," Trisha said. "We should get to know each other better, now that Nick hired Tilde to be his receptionist. We're practically family."

"Absolutely," Aunt Tilde jumped in before anyone could correct her. She gave Nick a wide smile, who did not look at all happy. "We are definitely practically family."

Chapter 10

I pushed open the doors to Redemption's public library, taking a moment to breathe in the familiar scents of paper, leather, and soft, comfy cushions. I always loved the library. As a child, it was one of my favorite places to visit, and it was no different now.

Especially when I saw Vi, looking like her usual bundle of contradictions, sitting behind the counter. She smiled and waved at me, and I responded with a quick wave before hurrying to the counter. Vi had been instrumental in helping me get to the bottom of Trisha's aunt's missing dog, and I was hoping she could do the same with this case.

After leaving Nick's office with a lot of mixed feelings (especially around the double date, which was apparently happening—oddly enough, Jerome had thought it sounded like a great idea when I asked him) and confusing thoughts, my mind kept circling back to Nick's warning.

I had a terrible feeling he was right, and we weren't going to be able to save Ruth's house. Which meant I had to put all my energy into making this transition as smooth as possible (assuming losing a house to unpaid property taxes could ever be smooth) for Ruth, and by extension, Aunt Tilde.

And that meant I was stuck trying to locate a stupid ghost.

Ugh. Some days, I really hated my job.

"So how do you find a ghost?" Nora had asked the day after we filled her in on the case. She and Smoke, her ill-tempered gray cat, were waiting for us at the agency, along with Scout, my yellow lab mix, and Sherlock, Aunt Tilde's little calico cat. Scout had been lying on his dog bed, but he had been giving Smoke the side-eye, who was glaring at him from the opposite side of the agency. Nora, as usual, was oblivious to the pet dynamics. She had attempted to braid her long, dark-red, frizzy hair, but the braids were starting to unravel at the ends. Her long mauve skirt hung on her too-thin frame, and her cream blouse was wrinkled. Her oversized glasses seemed to swallow her petite face as she blinked owlishly as Aunt Tilde and Mildred took turns telling her the story.

"An excellent question," Mildred said, adjusting her glasses and giving Aunt Tilde a hard look. "I'd love to hear the answer as well."

Aunt Tilde waved her hand. "Emily is going to let us know after she researches it."

I dropped the pen I was holding and looked at her in exasperation. "Seriously? That was your plan? That I would magically figure out a way to track down a missing ghost?"

Aunt Tilde had the grace to look slightly ashamed. "But you're so good at researching things. I figured you could handle it. Although," her expression shifted, and she looked suddenly sheepish, "I guess I was also sort of hoping Hank would … you know … show up again in a day or two."

"Fat chance of that happening," Mildred muttered.

Aunt Tilde looked at her in genuine surprise. "Why? Hank had appeared once before. Why wouldn't he again?"

Mildred raised her eyebrows. "You're kidding, right? It's obvious why Hank left."

I eyed both Nora and Aunt Tilde, but they looked as perplexed as I felt. Mildred looked around at our expressions and let out a loud sigh. "She's losing her home," she said, as if that explained everything.

It apparently did for Nora, because her face cleared. "Oh, you think Hank just moved out early."

Mildred frowned at her. "Hank didn't 'move out,' because Hank doesn't exist. But even if he did exist, he'd be a ghost. How much packing do you think he would need to do?"

"Well, he's lived there for a long time," Nora said. "Both as a human and as a ghost. I know it would take me months to pack, so I imagine trying to pack up both human and ghostly belongings would be completely overwhelming."

"I don't even want to think about trying to move," Aunt Tilde said. "Emily, I don't know how you did it. I think the only way I could do it is if I hired an organizer. And had a prescription for Valium." Aunt Tilde furrowed her brow. "But I don't think they have ghostly equivalents of either of those."

"I don't think Hank left because he was too frazzled at the thought of packing without drugs," I said, trying to get the conversation back on track. At the rate things were going, it would take all night to discuss various moving scenarios. "I think Mildred is trying to say something else."

"That's exactly right," Mildred said, nodding her head and shooting me an approving look.

There was an awkward pause as we all waited for Mildred to tell us what that reason was.

Mildred shook her head, her expression exasperated. "I can't believe you don't see it."

"Maybe we do," Aunt Tilde said. "We just want to hear you say it."

Mildred gave her a look. "Ruth is looking for an excuse not to be kicked out of her home. If the government tries to evict her, she's going to say she can't go, because her dead husband's ghost is missing, and if they kick her out, he won't be able to find her. Maybe she'll even take it a step further and say if Hank comes back and she's not there, he'll turn into an angry, vengeful ghost and take it out on the new unlucky owners. After all, who wants to live with an upset ghost?"

"Not me," Nora said with a shudder. "It was bad enough living with a sad one. I wasn't able to get a wink of sleep with all the moaning and chain-rattling going on."

Mildred looked at her incredulously. "Are you talking about that time you lived in the duplex next to that dominatrix?"

"Was that why your rent was so cheap?" Aunt Tilde asked her.

Nora wrinkled her nose. "Why do you think the ghost was so unhappy? She did not approve of what that dominatrix was doing. At all."

"So you think Ruth knew Hank wasn't real?" I asked, changing the subject and trying to ignore the rumblings in my stomach. With any luck, I could wrap up the current conversation before one of the other three decided we needed to continue the meeting over dinner.

Mildred sniffed. "Of course Ruth knew Hank the ghost wasn't real. She's a bit scattered and way too trusting. Otherwise, she never would have hired the gardener to be an accountant. But she's not an idiot."

"Ruth *isn't* an idiot," Aunt Tilde said.

"I know. I just said that," Mildred said.

"You just said she's an idiot if she thinks Hank is real," Aunt Tilde said.

"No, I said she's *not* an idiot, and she knows Hank isn't real," Mildred said.

"I don't agree," Aunt Tilde said.

Mildred looked puzzled. "So now you think she *is* an idiot?"

"No, I don't," Aunt Tilde said firmly.

"I think what Aunt Tilde is saying," I broke in, "is that Ruth does believe that Hank the ghost is real, but just because she believes that ghosts are real doesn't make her an idiot."

Mildred sat back and folded her arms across her chest. "Well, that's silly."

"It's an interesting idea," I said before Aunt Tilde could chime in. "That the reason Hank disappeared is linked to the property tax fiasco. It's possible you're both right—that Ruth does believe Hank is real, but her subconscious knows he's not, and to protect herself, she had Hank 'disappear.'" I put air quotes around the word "disappear."

"Oh, that's just a bunch of psychology gobbledygook," Mildred said. "Ruth knows the truth. She's probably just embarrassed about allowing herself to get scammed by her gardener."

"Actually, I think Emily has a point," Aunt Tilde said. "Mildred, you remember how Ruth was before Hank appeared? Those weeks after he died … she could barely get herself out of bed. She wasn't eating, wasn't showering. I really thought she might follow him to the grave."

"I remember," Mildred said, her face softening before her eyes flashed with anger. "It was awful. The media wouldn't leave her alone. And Redemption Manufacturing! They should be ashamed of themselves, the way they treated her. Not paying her Hank's full pension and giving her a settlement. Hank had been a loyal employee for years. Even if he did like to dabble with prostitutes, it shouldn't have mattered to Redemption Manufacturing."

"Exactly," Aunt Tilde said. "You, me, Lynne, and a few of her other friends did what we could, but poor Ruth must have felt so alone and betrayed by almost everyone. But after Hank returned, albeit as a ghost, everything changed. She was so much happier and obviously far less lonely."

"She also got another cat," Mildred said. "That probably helped her more than a pretend ghost."

"How can you be so sure Hank wasn't real?" Aunt Tilde asked.

"Because most ghosts aren't real," Mildred said.

I raised my eyebrow. "Most?"

"Well, there's always an exception," Mildred said.

"Who has been blinking the lights on and off to answer Ruth's questions, then?" Aunt Tilde asked.

"Probably electrical problems," Mildred said.

"Well, that may be true," Aunt Tilde said. "But it wasn't electrical problems that moved letters around on her fridge."

"Nor was it a ghost," Mildred said.

"Well, how do you explain it then?" Aunt Tilde said.

Mildred threw up her hands. "How should I know? Maybe the cat did it. Maybe she moved them around herself. Or maybe it was her gardener, playing a cruel game with her."

"She hasn't seen her gardener in months," Aunt Tilde said.

"Just because she hasn't seen him doesn't mean he hasn't been around," Mildred said.

Mildred had a point. It hadn't occurred to me that Bradley might be skulking around after apparently stealing Ruth's property taxes, but it was certainly a possibility.

"So going back to finding Hank," I said. "While I'm inclined to agree with Mildred that there is no ghost," Mildred had a smug look on her face, at that, "if Ruth really does believe Hank's ghost was living with her all these years and is now gone, we need to do something to either help her realize Hank's ghost is still with her or help her let him go."

"Or we could just find Hank," Nora said. "It can't be that hard to find a ghost. How far could he have gone? Aren't ghosts tethered to a location?"

"Only if they died there," Mildred said. "And Hank didn't die there. He died in that alley. So why isn't he haunting the alley? Another reason why I don't think he's real." She shot Aunt Tilde a meaningful look, who waved her off.

"Well, he can't have gone far," Nora said before furrowing her brow. "Could he?"

"Depends on how far he needed to go to buy cigarettes," Mildred said.

"I have another idea," I said. "What if, instead of trying to track down a ghost, we focus on helping Ruth find peace around Hank's death?"

"How do you propose we do that?" Aunt Tilde asked.

I took a deep breath. This idea had been circulating in my mind since Nick had given me his warning, but I wasn't sure how it would land. "What if we do our own investigation into how Hank died? You know, to see if we can find out what actually happened to him. If Ruth could learn the truth, it might give her a good deal of peace."

"I doubt she's going to feel much peace knowing her husband was spending money on prostitutes," Mildred said.

But I wasn't so sure. To me, there were enough questions and inconsistencies that it was worth looking into. Like, how was it that Hank's coworkers had told the cops they had seen him with a prostitute? How did they even know who the prostitutes were? And why were they hanging out in that area of town, unless they, too, were paying prostitutes? And if that were the case, then how was it that Hank was the only one who was killed that way? And if Hank had been paying prostitutes for years, why did he suddenly decide that day not to pay?

It made no sense.

And while the other three more or less agreed with me (Mildred was on the less side), they were all skeptical about anything being found after all this time.

"But isn't our motto 'Solving the Unsolvable?'" I asked Aunt Tilde.

"Yes, but ..." Aunt Tilde stuttered before finally sighing. "You got me. I guess, having lived through it all the first time, the idea of digging through all that unpleasantness again does not excite me. But you're right. There are questions, big ones, and we were aware of them when the cops did their initial investigation. They certainly haven't been answered since."

Which was how I found myself at the library, while Aunt Tilde, Nora, and Mildred researched ways to find ghosts.

I definitely had the better end of the deal.

"Emily, so nice to see you," Vi said with a big smile. She was about my age, maybe a few years older, with long, reddish-brown hair pulled back in a messy ponytail. She wore no makeup, but there was a tiny gold stud in her nose that matched her gold-rimmed glasses. She wore jeans, a button-down red shirt, and the same thick, brown cardigan she always wore, even though it was pretty hot for September. Although, because it was still hot outside, the air conditioning was cranked up to nearly arctic temperatures in the library, so the sweater made sense. "Are you here for another case?" She lowered her voice as she gave me a conspiratorial look, although there wasn't anyone in the library save for the old balding man sitting in the same spot he always sat in, with today's *Redemption Times* in front of him.

"It is," I said, keeping my voice low as well. "I'm looking into a cold case that happened about a decade back."

Vi's eyes lit up, and she scooted forward on her stool to lean closer to me. "Ooo, a real cold case. Was it here in Redemption?"

"It was."

"So you're going to want to check the newspaper files. Ten years ago, you say? Those articles are on microfilm, but I can show you how to use the machine. What's the case?"

I quickly gave her the high-level details, which she seemed shocked to hear. "Really? That happened in Redemption?" She furrowed her brow. "Oh, but you said it was ten years ago. I would have been at school then, which is probably why I don't remember it. Well, let's see what the *Redemption Times* had to say about it." She pushed away from the counter and led me to the back of the library where the microfiche machines were located, along with the files of films.

As usual, I didn't know the exact date. Aunt Tilde thought it had happened in June or July, whereas Mildred was sure it was in November, right around Thanksgiving. Although that didn't sound right, why would anyone be engaging with a prostitute outside in November? But when Aunt Tilde brought that up, Mildred insisted that was why she remembered the date … because she was in the middle of planning a dish she was making for Thanksgiving, and her first thought was that maybe Hank should be trussed up like a turkey. Nora, on the other hand, was sure it was sometime in the spring, as it was around the same time she got Smoke. Or maybe she got Smoke a few years later on the anniversary of Hank's murder. Either way, she was sure it had happened in the spring.

"Let's just start at the beginning of 1983," I said, crossing my fingers that at minimum, the year would be correct. At least in this case, unlike the last one, I would only have to look at the front page, so it should make going through the papers faster.

A couple of hours later, I had a terrible crick in my neck and the beginnings of a headache thudding through my temples, but I had hit pay dirt. To my utter surprise, it turned out Nora was the one who was right—Hank died in the beginning of April. The week before Easter, to be precise, which might also explain Mildred and the turkey, if she was planning on cooking a turkey for Easter dinner.

Needless to say, the story was front-page news for over a week with a few follow-up articles published several weeks later. The cops had glommed onto the prostitution angle, but they were unable to locate the correct prostitute. The prostitutes they dragged into the station swore up and down they didn't know a thing, and the one Hank's coworkers had seen him with had gone missing. While the cops didn't officially close the case, it appeared that it eventually got relegated to the cold-case files. It also appeared that because the investigation was so lacking, much of the "reporting" sounded like it should have been regulated to the gossip pages.

"I always knew there was something off with him," one of his coworkers, an unpleasant-sounding woman named Karen Crabtree, had proclaimed. "It was the eyes. They were shifty."

At that, I examined the small black-and-white photo of Hank that had accompanied the story. If his eyes were shifty in real life, they sure weren't in the picture. He looked like any other middle-aged accountant in a suit, hair combed over his bald spot, and a smile that appeared more of a grimace. To me, he didn't look at all like a man who was sneaking off to see prostitutes.

But as much as I wanted it to be otherwise, I couldn't ignore how bad it looked for Hank. And it wasn't just because he was found in an alley that was known to be frequented by prostitutes with his pants down.

For years, Hank had worked late. Not at the office, but somewhere else. At least that's what he told some of his male colleagues, who would ask him from time to time to have drinks with them after work. He would occasionally go out with them, but mostly, he would say he couldn't because of his other job. It was all very mysterious, and even before his scandalous death, there had been a lot of rumors flying about what precisely he was doing. And of course, the fact he was seen at the Lone Man Standing, a bar notorious for gang activity, drug dealing, and, yes, prostitution, only fueled the speculation. Some thought he had a second job working for the gang. Others thought he actually worked for the government—maybe as a CIA or FBI agent—and was gathering evidence for them. (That rumor had me examining his photo again, trying to see if I could get a glimpse into this man with a double life. Alas, he still looked like a boring middle-aged accountant.)

Hank, for his part, would merely say it was nothing—he was helping a few friends out with their books. There was no conflict with Redemption Manufacturing, just as long as it wasn't another manufacturing company, and no one seemed to think it was.

But still, it was odd. Where else was he working? After his death, no "friends" came out to say Hank had helped them with their books. Was it the Lone Man Standing? If it were, the newspaper didn't say one way or another. Nor did any of the police officers they had quoted in the article. I wondered if the police would let me look at their files, but I had a sneaking suspicion they would not. And, as the Lone Man Standing had unfortunately burned down five years before, I couldn't go to the horse's mouth.

Redemption Manufacturing had issued a terse statement basically saying that whatever Hank was involved in, it was on his own time, and it wasn't a reflection of the company or its employees. It was implied that if Redemption Manufacturing had known about Hank's extracurricular activities, they would have fired him. And considering they had taken away Ruth's pension, I had no doubt they would have fired him. I also suspected they would be less than thrilled to answer a few questions for me.

So now what? I pushed away from the microfiche machine and began kneading my temples, attempting to rebuff the headache. It wasn't working, so I dug through my purse for the aspirin I always carried before getting up to locate a drinking fountain. I was hoping once my headache subsided, my next steps would be obvious, but I didn't think that was going to be the case. The only lead I had (although "lead" was probably overstating it) was a woman named MaryBeth Lassoon. She was one of Hank's coworkers, but unlike everyone else who seemed quick to throw Hank under the bus, she was far more subdued and respectful.

She was one of the women who had seen Hank at lunch with a prostitute. Her quote was, "Yes, I saw Hank with her, but I didn't see anything improper. It looked to me like he was simply buying her lunch, and based on how thin she was, she probably needed it."

Compared to all the other quotes, it was practically a full-throated defense of Hank.

I knew it was probably a long shot, but after I had taken my aspirin, I located a phone book. There was only one Lassoon with the first initial M.

Sounded promising. I scribbled the address and phone number in my notebook. I had no idea if she would talk to me, but it was worth a shot.

And if this idea didn't work, I had no idea what I would do next.

Chapter 11

"I'm so glad you found me," MaryBeth said as she placed a pot of tea in the middle of the round kitchen table covered with a cheery yellow and white tablecloth. Actually, her entire kitchen was cheery, with sparkling white appliances, yellow curtains, and orange and yellow roosters decorating everything. It even smelled clean, of lemon polish and soap.

MaryBeth appeared to be in her mid-seventies, although she was in excellent shape. Her white hair was thin and sparse, and her face was wrinkled with splotches of sun damage, but her grip when she shook my hand was stronger than I expected. She wore a crisp blouse covered with blue and yellow flowers and pressed yellow slacks. She immediately ushered me into the kitchen, where she laid out freshly baked banana bread and tea. Outside the window overlooking the kitchen table, I could see an older man, who I assumed was her husband, puttering around the very large flower garden.

"I'm glad you're willing to talk to me," I said, taking a sip of the tea. It was floral and sweet. I couldn't place the individual flavors, but it was very good.

"Of course. I always felt so terrible for poor Ruth. I'm glad you're looking into what happened. Lord knows the cops did an awful job." She shook her head as she pushed the plate of banana bread toward me. "How is she, by the way?"

"She's okay," I said, deciding I didn't need to get into the whole "she might lose her house" backstory. Or even worse, the whole "her husband's ghost went missing, as well."

"Yes, I'm sure it's rough for her." She sighed sadly, picking up her teacup. "I don't know what I'd do with myself without my Fred. He's always been my rock. And I had a job for years ... unlike Ruth, who basically devoted her life to taking care of Hank."

"I think it's been pretty rough for her," I said. Considering she had convinced herself that her husband's ghost was still living with her, I thought that was a fairly truthful statement. "If I can get to the bottom of what happened to Hank, I'm hoping to bring her some closure … maybe even some peace."

"Oh, for Ruth's sake, I hope you succeed." She reached for the sugar and dropped a cube into her cup. "You know, I retired not long after Hank was murdered."

"I didn't know that." Although looking at her, it made sense. She would have been in her mid-sixties back then, which would definitely be retirement age.

She nodded slowly as she stirred her tea. "It was already in motion before Hank, but if it hadn't been, I still would have retired. I was so disgusted by how Redemption Manufacturing handled the whole sordid mess. And my coworkers! What a pack of jackals."

I was a little taken aback—not so much by what she said, but by the venomous tone she said it in. My first impression of MaryBeth was that she was a sweet old woman, which she very well might be, but there was a spine of steel beneath the sugar coating.

"Yeah, the quotes in the articles weren't very … kind." I wasn't sure if that was the right word, but it was the only one that came to mind.

She let out a bitter snort of laughter. "That's a very polite understatement. Your mother must have raised you well." I pressed my lips together at that. As far as I was concerned, she hadn't raised me at all. I was the one who had taken care of her, as she spent most of my childhood in an alcoholic haze, but that was neither here nor there. "Ghouls, is what they were. Couldn't get enough of the gossip and rumors. You would have thought Hank was the worst villain in a superhero movie, rather than a decent man who kept to himself and quietly did his job."

"So you don't believe he was sleeping with prostitutes?" I asked.

She made that snorting noise again. "Heavens no. He worshipped Ruth. He would never have cheated on her." She sounded so sure of herself that I almost believed her. That is, until I remembered all the circumstantial evidence against him.

"Do you have a theory as to why he was found in such a … compromising situation?" I asked.

She paused, looking away and toward the window that overlooked the backyard where her husband was. But I didn't think she was seeing her husband. I had a feeling she was lost in the past. "That is the million-dollar question. To this day, it continues to vex me. Sometimes, I lie awake at night and try to puzzle through what he was thinking or doing." She started blinking her eyes rapidly, and I realized there was a sheen in them, almost like tears. She put her teacup on the table and picked up a napkin to dab at her eyes. "I worked with Hank in the accounting department. For years, we worked side by side. We didn't talk much—like I said, Hank kept to himself, which I respected. I didn't like getting involved in office politics either. But we talked enough that I felt like I knew him. I considered us friends. Maybe not best friends, but … friends. Of course, I knew he had a side job. He didn't talk about it much, but I knew. He told me he was doing it for Ruth. He wanted to make sure she was taken care of, no matter what, so he was trying to save as much money as possible. And that made sense. Hank rarely spent money on clothes, and Ruth always made him a lunch to bring to work. He certainly never acted like a man who would waste money on hookers. But …" she shook her head and absentmindedly stirred her tea. "I can't explain it. Any of the rumors. Why he was at the Lone Man Standing? Why was he with Jazzy that day?"

I tilted my head. "Jazzy?"

She wasn't looking at me. Rather, she continued staring into her cup. "The young prostitute he was with a few days before he died. The one no one could find."

"You knew her?"

She took the spoon out of her teacup and placed it on the table. "I used to volunteer for a nonprofit organization called The Dawn of Hope, which is all about helping teenage runaways get off the streets. Jazzy was one of the ones we were trying to help. I don't know her real name … only knew her as Jazzy. She was a little older than the ones we usually helped—nearly twenty, if I recall, though it's possible she had lied to us about her age."

I couldn't believe what I was hearing. MaryBeth knew the prostitute Hank had been with a few days before his murder. "Did you tell the cops?"

Her eyes shifted to mine. "Of course I did. Do you think they cared? Not a chance." Her voice was bitter.

"I don't understand. Why wouldn't they?"

"Because she was disposable. Like all those young prostitutes. They didn't care about her. They only cared that they couldn't *find* her. She disappeared after Hank was killed. The cops assumed she was the one who had killed Hank, and that she had robbed him and run off. When they couldn't find her, they just stopped looking. I think they all thought Hank deserved it on some level. If he hadn't been messing around with prostitutes, he never would have gotten himself killed." Her voice had been getting louder and louder, and with some effort, she forced herself to stop and take a breath. "Sorry. I still get so angry every time I think about it. It's so upsetting, how those poor girls, and even boys, are treated. Like they're less than human. And therefore, no one can be bothered."

"So even though Jazzy disappeared after Hank was killed, you don't think she had anything to do with his death?"

"I didn't say that," MaryBeth said.

I blinked. "Wait. You do think she was responsible?"

MaryBeth shook her head. "Not responsible. No, I never believed that. But had something to do with it?" She moved her head from side to side. "Maybe. It's possible."

"Do you have any theories?"

"None that make sense." She paused and picked up her teacup, cupping it in her hands as if to absorb the warmth. "Jazzy had a terrible pimp. It was one of the reasons why we had so many difficulties getting her off the streets. Drake was vicious and violent. He had a reputation for tracking down any girl who tried to leave him and either dragging her back to the streets or … well, punishing her severely. Trying to free a girl in his clutches was a very delicate operation. Jean, that's who was running the foundation back then, was worried sick about Jazzy."

"So what happened to her?"

MaryBeth sighed. "No one knows. The last person to see her alive that I know of was Hank, the day he bought her lunch. That was certainly the last time I saw her. At that point, Jean hadn't seen her for over a week." She looked down into her mug. "I could see her black eye and split lip from across the restaurant, even though she had tried to cover it with makeup. I almost approached her ... them. I really wanted to. But I was with another coworker at the time, and I was afraid all I would do was scare Jazzy away. She was always very skittish, ready to run at the slightest thing. But I told myself at least she was eating something nutritious, and she was safe, for the moment. I thought it was best to just let it be."

"But ..." I was trying to figure out how to word my question without offending her. "I mean, weren't you at least a little concerned for her? I know you considered Hank a friend, but he was having lunch with a prostitute. Didn't it at least occur to you that something else might be going on?"

Her eyes flicked up toward me. "Of course it did. I'm not a fool. But ..." she paused, working her mouth as if she was trying to figure out how to word her answer. "There was no reason for Hank to buy her lunch. If he just wanted to ... have sex with her, all he had to do was pay her. He didn't need to sit next to her in public while she ate a sandwich. And only she was eating, in case that wasn't clear. He wasn't eating, and later that afternoon, I saw him in the break-room scarfing down the lunch Ruth packed him. So, he had spent his lunch break not only not eating, but paying for someone else's lunch and watching her eat. Remember, this was a man who rarely, if ever, ate out or even had a drink after work, so for him to have bought Jazzy lunch ..."

She hesitated, almost as if she had more to say but wasn't sure if she should or not, but after a moment, she continued. "This might sound a little silly, but watching them ... the vibe I got was more of a father buying lunch for his daughter. It was very paternal energy. Not ... well, like a man who was interested in something else."

"Did you ever ask him about Jazzy?"

She didn't answer immediately. In fact, she took such a long time to answer, I almost repeated my question, certain she hadn't heard me. But there was something about her expression, something uncomfortable and awkward. It was so at odds with what she had told me, I had to force myself to stay quiet and give her space to figure it out.

Finally, she let out a long breath. "I did. But … I don't know if I want to talk about it."

I could hear alarm bells going off in my head. Listening to her talk about Hank and Jazzy, I was starting to wonder if maybe the police had gotten everything backwards, and Hank was trying to help Jazzy, but something had gone very wrong. At this point, I didn't know what to think. "Look, all I'm trying to do is get to the bottom of what happened to Hank. I'm not the police, or a journalist. No one is going to jail. And I don't even have to tell Ruth if it turns out it's … not going to help her. But if you know something, it could really help make my life a lot easier."

She let out a long sigh. "It's just … it's going to sound like I was a fool."

I stared at her. "I don't understand."

She put her mug back on the table. "The thing is, when I asked Hank, his reaction … look I never told anyone this. Not even Fred."

"I don't need to tell anyone either," I said.

She raised her eyes and searched my face. I wasn't sure what she was seeing, but her expression relaxed slightly, and she gave a little nod. "When I approached Hank, he was in the breakroom getting another cup of coffee. There was no one else there, so I thought it was a good time. I asked him about Jazzy, and his face … his face just went completely white. Immediately, before I could even finish what I was going to say, he was denying it. Said I must have been mistaken. It took me aback. I had been trying to tell him about The Dawn of Hope and how we had been trying to help Jazzy get off the streets, but I don't think it came out right. He just kept saying I must have been mistaken, as he didn't know anyone by that name. And then someone else came into the breakroom, and that was it. He quickly left with his coffee, and a couple of days later, he was dead."

I stared at her, trying to fit this new information into the rest of what MaryBeth had told me. "That's so … odd."

She swallowed hard. "I know. It feels disloyal to even say it, but …" She straightened up and looked me right in the eyes. "He was acting guilty. Like maybe he had been hiring her for sex."

There was a long moment as I pondered her words. The whole time, as I had listened to MaryBeth, I was so sure it was key to proving he hadn't been hiring prostitutes, and there was another explanation for his death. But now …

"To be clear, I still don't believe it. I can't explain any of it. Not why he bought lunch for Jazzy, or that last conversation, or why he ended up in that alley. All I can say is, my gut is sure he didn't do any of it. But …" a faint smile touched her lips. "I understand my gut is hardly proof. And I knew if I told anyone about that last conversation, they would immediately dismiss anything else I said."

"Did the cops even ask you if you asked Hank about Jazzy?" I asked.

Her eyes were steady on mine. "I told them I was waiting for the right time to ask Hank, when there wasn't anyone else around. Which wasn't entirely a lie. I *was* waiting for the right time to bring it up again. I couldn't believe Hank had been hiring Jazzy, and I had been trying to think of another way of approaching the subject with him. Unfortunately, I ran out of time."

Man, I truly wish she hadn't run out of time. I felt like I had taken two steps forward and three steps back. Maybe Mildred had been right all along. "And you never saw Jazzy again?"

She shook her head. "Never."

"What about her pimp? Drake, was it?"

She pressed her mouth to together. "Unfortunately, yes. Although he's dead now. Died a couple of years ago. A bullet to the back of the head. Took a while, but finally, he angered the wrong person."

My shoulders slumped. Not that I wanted Drake to be alive; it sounded like everyone was better off with him dead. But that also meant no one could ask him about Hank. "Did you ever think he might have killed Hank?"

I'm not sure what I was expecting. I just tossed the question out there, but MaryBeth's expression turned serious. "Many times. Especially if it turned out Hank was trying to help Jazzy. I could totally see Drake killing him." She made a face. "Of course, I could also see Drake kill Hank if Hank was trying to screw Jazzy by not paying her."

"What about The Dawn of Hope? Could I talk to them?" I felt like I was grasping at straws, but what else could I do?

"You could, but Jean isn't there anymore. She left and moved to Florida a few years back."

Ugh. Another lead gone. "Do you have her number, or any way to contact her?"

She shook her head. "No, by the time she moved, I wasn't volunteering anymore. After what happened to Hank, Fred didn't want me involved. Said it was too dangerous. We still donate money though. I can give you their contact information. They might be able to help you get in touch with Jean."

I nodded, despite it feeling like a long shot. "Thank you. That would be great." I forced a smile on my face, even though I was feeling discouraged and hopeless. If this were the story from a woman who truly thought Hank was innocent, I didn't even want to think about what the rest of my investigation would uncover. Probably hard proof that Hank was every bit the cheating jerk everyone seemed to think he was.

Chapter 12

"Isn't this fun?" Trisha gushed as we settled into our seats at Mario's, Redemption's premier (and also only) Italian restaurant. It was also more upscale, with its white tablecloths and fat white candles stuffed in wine bottles covered with straw.

"I agree! This was a great idea," Jerome said, smiling enthusiastically as he gave my arm a quick squeeze. "We should have thought of it sooner."

No, we shouldn't have. The words were on the tip of my tongue, but I forced myself to swallow them and flash him a tight smile instead. The only thing I was enthusiastic about was the meal. Mario's had become my favorite restaurant in Redemption, so I at least knew I would enjoy the food.

Jerome must have interpreted my strained smile as encouragement because he turned back to Trisha. "We'll be the ones to plan the next date."

Next? We hadn't even gotten through this one yet. I hadn't even ordered my wine yet. Why would he make such a promise? At least the wine part was going to be righted soon, as I could see our waiter was on his way over.

I wondered whether ordering a bottle would be in poor taste, although I almost immediately decided against it. Everyone would assume I was getting it for the table rather than myself.

"This is one of our favorites," Trisha said, once the appetizer, fried calamari, was ordered. She hugged Nick's arm, beaming up at him. My stomach twisted in an uncomfortable knot, and despite being famished when we walked in, I was no longer hungry. As usual, Trisha looked spectacular. Her black hair hung loosely in thick curls over her shoulders, framing her high cheekbones and dark-blue eyes. Her lips were painted in a dark red that perfectly matched her silk, V-neck blouse. "Isn't that right, Nicky?"

Nicky? Ugh. How fast could the waiter get back with that wine? Would it be too obnoxious if I got up and helped myself at the bar?

"Mario's always does a good job," Nick said. Was it my imagination, or did he look as pained as I felt? His green eyes flickered in the candlelight, and just like that, his expression became unreadable again.

"It's one of our favorites, too," Jerome said, slinging an arm across the back of my chair. "We had our first date here, didn't we?"

"We did," I said, with a far more genuine smile for Jerome.

Just then, the table jerked. "Sorry about that," Nick said, shifting in his chair.

Trisha laughed, her little tinkling laugh. "You can be such a klutz, Nicky."

I tried not to wince. Every time she called him that, it was like nails on a chalkboard. It was going to be a long night if that kept up.

"Well, if they didn't make these tables so small, I wouldn't kick them accidentally," Nick said with a trace of his old grin. "You know what I'm talking about, don't you, Jeremiah?"

"It's Jerome," Jerome said.

Nick's smile widened slightly as he smacked himself on the side of the head. "Oh, of course. Sorry. I don't know why I keep doing that."

Trisha playfully bopped him on the arm. "It's probably because you work so hard. You need a better assistant than ..." she glanced up, giving me a guilty look. "Well, sorry, Emily."

"Why are you sorry?" I asked as the waiter appeared with our drinks.

"Well, because she's your aunt and all," Trisha said as she reached for her white wine spritzer. Of course that would be Trisha's type of drink.

"My aunt?" I stared at her in bewilderment. "My aunt doesn't work for Nick." I glanced at Nick, expecting him to back me up, but he just looked uncomfortable as he took a swig of beer.

"Yes, she does. Why else would she be sitting at the reception desk?" Trisha asked.

"She was just making a call that day," I said.

"But then why was she digging around in the desk?" Trisha asked.

Ugh. Maybe I should just admit my aunt was a snoop and leave it at that.

"Tilde does a few odd jobs for me from time to time," Nick said before I could open my mouth.

I shut it with a click. "Excuse me? She does what?"

Nick shrugged as he picked up his beer again, not exactly meeting my eyes. "I thought you knew."

"How could I know? Why would she do that when she has The Redemption Detective Agency?"

He finally met my gaze. "You know she doesn't make any money with that."

I bristled. He was laughing at me; I could see it in his eyes. Did he honestly think I didn't know that? All I did every day was try to bring money in the door of that place, never mind turn a profit. "And you pay her?"

That wiped the humor off his face. "Well, no …"

"So, she's volunteering her time to be your receptionist?"

"Not exactly," Nick said. He gave Trisha the side-eye, and I could almost hear his thoughts—*see what you did?* "Tilde knows I've had trouble … filling that position. So, she comes in from time to time to help me stay organized."

My eyes widened. Aunt Tilde was helping Nick be organized? No wonder his office looked like it was hit by a tornado. "You can't be serious."

The laughter came back into his eyes. "Well, not everyone can have the great Emily, Office Manager Extraordinaire, in charge."

Trisha tapped one of her manicured nails against her wineglass. I noticed they were painted red to match her lipstick, and her lipstick was now smeared on her glass. "Oh, that's a great idea, Nicky! You should hire Emily to organize your office."

I nearly spat out my wine. "Wait, what?"

"Emily has a job," Jerome said tightly. I had been so focused on Nick, I'd nearly forgotten he was there. I gave him a weak smile and hoped it wasn't obvious.

"Yeah, I don't know if that's such a great idea, Trish," Nick said.

"Why not?" Trisha asked, seeming oblivious of the energy around the table. "She's much more organized than Tilde." She raised her eyebrows. "Not to mention her outfits are better."

I could feel my cheeks grow warm. I was wearing one of my favorite shirts, a lavender, sleeveless blouse with a jewel neckline, paired with a heavy gold necklace and gold hoops, but based on the way Trisha's eyes raked over my clothes, she didn't think much of my ensemble.

Or, I should say, she thought I was better dressed than my eccentric, flamboyant aunt. Which was a pretty low bar, at least according to her.

"I still don't understand why Aunt Tilde is working for you," I said. "As you pointed out, she already has one job that doesn't pay. Why would she need two?"

"She's doing it as a trade for my legal help," Nick said. "I don't feel right charging her," Trisha rolled her eyes at that, "but she doesn't feel right accepting my help for free. So, we compromised."

"But she makes everyone else work for free at The Redemption Agency." *Except for me*, I added in my head. It wasn't a regular paycheck, though, nor did I feel at all comfortable with the arrangement. But if a client decided to give us money, I was the one who typically ended up with it, as Aunt Tilde assured me everyone else had other streams of income they could rely on. I was determined to change that dynamic and make sure everyone got paid, but first, I had to convince Aunt Tilde to actually start charging clients.

"I'm not talking about the agency work," he said. "I'm talking about her real estate business."

I blinked at him. *Real estate business?*

He must have seen something in my eyes because he looked uncomfortable. "Oh, I thought you knew."

"Aunt Tilde has a real estate business?" I asked.

He was watching me carefully. "You never wondered how she got the money to dump into The Redemption Detective Agency?"

"I ..." I stopped, feeling like an idiot. Of course I wondered, but I had assumed she had some sort of pension from her job as a nurse at the hospital, and maybe some investments had done well. Well, if I were being honest, I also assumed she might have some less-than-legal sources of money, and the less I knew about that, the better. The image of Aunt Tilde's Mary Kay pink Cadillac floated through my head. I never did get an answer as to how she ended up with that car.

Luckily, at that moment, the waiter arrived with our appetizer and asked if we wanted to order. I hadn't even looked at the menu, so I ordered the chicken parmesan, one of my favorites, along with another glass of wine, even though I hadn't finished the first one yet.

I had a feeling this was going to be a long night.

I was still mulling over Aunt Tilde and wondering what else I didn't know about her (and did that make me a terrible niece?) when Trisha leaned forward toward Jerome, which allowed Jerome a good look at her ample bosom. "So, you work at the school, right?"

"I do," Jerome said. He was trying hard not to look at what Trisha was putting on display, and I had to give him credit for almost succeeding. Although I wondered why Nick didn't put a stop to it. I peeked at him from the bottom of my lashes and noticed his brooding expression as he stared into his beer. "I taught chemistry, and now, I'm the principal."

Trisha's eyes lit up. "That's what I thought. And that makes you the exact person I need to talk to. I have some questions."

"Well, I have answers. Hopefully, correct ones." He smiled self-consciously at his joke, still doing a gallant job of not looking at Trisha's breasts. "Do you have children in our school district?"

Trisha tittered. "No, not yet. Although someday, I hope to." She batted her eyelashes at Nick, who didn't look amused. She pouted slightly and turned back to Jerome. "But I do love children, and I definitely want to hear more about the educational opportunities in Redemption."

Jerome brightened. "Oh, that's wonderful to hear. And, while I'm more than happy to talk about our school district, since you don't have children yet, you might be interested in learning about some other volunteer opportunities that are available here in Redemption. There are so many children who would benefit, even if you can only spare a few hours a month. I can tell you from experience that Big Brothers, Big Sisters is a fabulous organization, and they're always looking for volunteers …"

"Yes, yes, I'm sure they're great," Trisha interrupted, waving her hand. "I really wanted to hear more about the school itself, though … especially if any volunteer opportunities are available there."

Jerome's brows knitted together. "I'm not sure I understand. You want to volunteer at our school?"

"Oh, not me," Trisha said with her little laugh again. "It's for my cousin. She just moved to Redemption."

"Oh." Jerome's expression cleared. "Of course. How old are her children?"

"Oh, she doesn't have children," Trisha said. "At least, not yet. But she definitely wants a big family."

Jerome's brows knitted together. "Wait, she doesn't have children either?"

"She's still looking for that special someone," Trisha explained, tucking her hand in the spot between Nick's arm and his side. "Unfortunately, she hasn't been lucky in that department … not like the four of us."

"It's tough out there," Jerome said, putting his arm around me and giving me a squeeze as he smiled at me. I smiled back. He really was a good guy.

"Aww, you guys are so sweet," Trisha said. She was smiling, but Nick's face was expressionless. He reached for his beer. "I'm glad you two found each other."

"So am I," Jerome said, letting go of me to reach for his own beer. "So, your cousin is looking for volunteer opportunities working with kids?"

"Exactly, at the school," Trisha said.

Jerome frowned. "I'm not sure if I know of any organizations that meet at the school. I think most of them use the library or conference room at the Redemption Inn."

"No, I'm talking about volunteering with the school itself," Trisha said. "You know, like helping out in classrooms, or maybe serving on the PTA?"

Jerome looked confused again. "Your cousin wants to volunteer for the … Parent Teacher Association?"

"Well, sure, that would work," Trisha said.

Jerome gave her a strange look. "The PTA stands for the *Parent Teacher* Association."

"Oh, yes, I knew that." Trisha tittered again and drained her wine. "So how would she get involved?"

Jerome hesitated, looking like he was trying to find the right words. "Normally, the PTA is only for parents."

"But it's not just for parents," Trisha said. "It's for teachers, too."

"Well, yes, but it would be … highly unusual for someone to join who didn't have a child attending the school."

"But surely there are things that need doing," Trisha said. "Teachers especially would be happy to have the extra help, I'm sure. They're so overworked anyway, and underpaid. Not that that's your fault," she added quickly. "It's just the way it is."

"Well, yes, that's true … but I still don't think I understand why she wants to volunteer at a school if she doesn't have children there."

"Eventually, she hopes her children will be students there," Trisha said. "After she meets the right someone. And I would think the PTA would be a great way to meet people in the community, wouldn't you?"

"Um …" Jerome's voice trailed off, seemingly too perplexed by the conversation to even respond. "I don't know if the PTA is really the place to pick up a … date."

"Why not?" Trisha asked. Her voice seemed sincere—like she really did think it was perfectly acceptable to join the PTA as a means to finding a husband. "I think that would be a great place to meet potential dates! You would already know you had something in common; you both want kids."

"I guess so …" Jerome said slowly. "I never really thought of it like that before."

Trisha's eyes lit up, and she let go of Nick's arm so she could gesture with her hands. "Like, I just met a new teacher the other day. Matthew Graves, I believe it was. Do you know who I'm talking about?"

"Um … yes …" Jerome said hesitantly.

Trisha leaned forward. "Do you know whether he's single or not? I didn't see a wedding ring, but that doesn't mean he's not with someone. I think he would be perfect for my cousin. Don't you think so?" she elbowed Nick, who had a pained look on his face.

"I'm not even sure I know which cousin you're talking about," Nick said.

Trisha glared at him. "What are you talking about? Of course you do. I have only one cousin who is moving to Redemption."

"Okay, but I also don't know this teacher, Matthew, at all, so I'm not going to be much help here," Nick said.

Trisha rolled her eyes. "Ugh … men. You're no help, period." She turned back to Jerome. "So, is he single?"

"That would be a … highly inappropriate question to ask him as the principal of his new school, so alas, I do *not* know," Jerome said.

Trisha made a face. "Great. I guess I'm going to have to figure it out on my own." She thought for a second before perking up. "Can you at least tell me when the next PTA meeting is? I'll just pop in as an interested volunteer and ask him myself."

Jerome gave her a pained look before opening his mouth, probably to try to explain again that a PTA meeting was not really an appropriate place for either her or her cousin to volunteer, when a familiar voice came from behind me. "What about this table? I can just sit here."

I whirled around to see Nora seating herself at the table next to us. "Nora?" I gasped. "What are you doing here?"

Nora widened her eyes in a completely over-the-top surprised expression. "Emily! I wasn't expecting to see you here tonight. What a coincidence."

"Ma'am," the hostess interrupted. She was young, maybe late teens or early twenties, with long brown hair that hung halfway down the back of her simple black dress. "I can take you to your table." She gestured toward the back of the restaurant.

"Oh, that's okay. I can stay here," Nora said cheerfully. The hostess looked nonplussed but handed her the menu and disappeared with a flounce.

"Nora, what are you doing here?" I hissed. I had been so careful to make sure no one knew where we were going.

"Having dinner," Nora said. "Just like you." She had dressed up for the occasion in a brightly colored beaded skirt and purple blousy top. It was quite a departure from the normal dull colors she typically wore. I had no idea she even had such vibrant items in her closet.

Nora peered over my shoulder and made a big show of pretending to notice I was at a table of four. "Oh, you've got company. Don't mind me. Carry on."

"Did Mildred tell you to come here?" I asked as she stared digging in the giant purse she had brought with her.

"Why would Mildred tell me to have dinner here?" Nora asked. Her voice was muffled as she continued rummaging around. "Oh, where is it? I'm sure I grabbed it."

I turned to Jerome, who shook his head. "Don't look at me. I didn't breathe a word."

"Who's that?" Trisha asked.

"Oh, I'm Nora," Nora said, her head popping out of the purse. In one hand, she held a small notebook and a pen. "I think we've met before. I'm a detective at The Redemption Detective Agency."

Trisha tapped her finger against her lips. "Oh, yeah. I think I remember you now. You're the one with the ornery cat."

"Smoke isn't ornery," Nora said, opening the notebook and uncapping her pen. "He's a very particular cat who likes to get his way."

"Don't we all?" Nick murmured, meeting my eyes. His expression was somewhere between amused and exasperated.

"Yes, well, he's in a particularly foul mood because I left him home, so I'm going to do something special for him," Nora said, sounding a little put-out.

"I'm surprised you didn't bring him with you," Nick said gravely.

Nora made a face. "It wasn't my idea. I tried to get them to let me bring him in with me, but they refused. Said something about health violations or something." She rolled her eyes.

"Nora, why do you have a notebook and pen?" I asked.

Nora glanced down, as if to remind herself of what was in her hand. "Oh, this. Well, you know, I thought I'd doodle a bit while I wait for dinner."

I gave her a skeptical look. "I've never seen you doodle."

Nora laughed nervously. "What do you mean? I doodle all the time." She quickly sketched something and showed it to me. "See?"

I squinted at the paper. It appeared to be a stickman. At least I think it was supposed to be a stick man. It seemed to have three feet and one arm.

Jerome leaned over my shoulder. "Is that a Dodo bird?"

"No, it's an elephant," Trisha said, also leaning over to see. She pointed to the drawing. "That's its trunk."

"Oh, I see it now," Jerome said, nodding.

"It's not an elephant. It's a house. Can't you see it?" Nora asked. She started gesturing toward her drawing, explaining where the chimney, door, and windows were, until thankfully, we were interrupted by our food and a fresh round of drinks arriving.

"So, about the PTA," Trisha said as she poked at her antipasto salad after looking longingly at Jerome's Fettuccini Alfredo. "When is their next meeting?"

Jerome mumbled something, but as his mouth was full of pasta, it was impossible to understand him.

"What did he say?" Nora asked, pen poised over her notebook.

"I thought you were doodling," I said.

Nora's eyes widened as she started scribbling over the page. "I *am* doodling."

"I don't know their meeting schedule off the top of my head, but again, as neither of you have kids, I'm not sure how appropriate it would be," Jerome said after swallowing his food.

Trisha did that little hand wave again. "It's only temporary. Once we're both settled, we'll have lots of kids."

"Who's having kids?" Nora asked.

"No one is having kids," I said.

"Not yet, at least," Trisha said.

"Not yet? What does that mean?" Nora asked, her brow furrowing. "Emily, are you pregnant?"

"What? No! Don't doodle that anywhere," I yelped, nearly jumping out of my chair to grab her notebook away from her. All I needed was to have Mildred and Aunt Tilde think I was pregnant.

"Well, what does 'not yet' mean, other than someone is pregnant?" Nora asked.

"No one is pregnant, and Trisha just means at some point over the next decade, she'll have a baby," I said.

Nora gave me a suspicious look. "You know, it's possible to be pregnant and not know it."

"I'm not pregnant," I said through gritted teeth. My face was hot, and I was sure I was beet red. I could practically feel both Nick and Jerome's eyes on me, and I refused to acknowledge either of them.

Nora still didn't look convinced. Instead, she started scribbling more frantically in her notebook. It was all I could do to keep myself from demanding to see what she was writing.

"I'll find out when the next PTA meeting is," Jerome said with a sigh as he sent me a sympathetic look. "Can I give you a call in the next day or so?"

Trisha beamed. "Absolutely. Thank you so much."

Nora's eyes narrowed, and she pointed her pen at me. "You ARE pregnant, aren't you? Otherwise, why would you want to go to a PTA meeting?"

I put my head in my hands and wished the floor would open up beneath me.

Chapter 13

"Isn't there something you want to tell us?" Mildred asked me as she poured herself a cup of coffee, a gleam in her eyes.

"Why yes," I said, putting my own coffee mug down on my desk with a thunk. "Ask you, really. Why did you send Nora to spy on us yesterday?"

Mildred widened her eyes as she attempted (and failed) to look innocent. "What are you talking about? It's not my fault Nora had a hankering for Italian food."

I narrowed my eyes. "How did you even know Nora was at the same restaurant I was if you hadn't sent her?"

"Oh, so you had a hankering for Italian food as well?" Mildred asked. "What a coincidence."

Ugh. "Nora could have made spaghetti at home if she had a hankering for Italian food. She certainly didn't need to go to Mario's for that."

"She might, though, if she wanted something other than spaghetti, like lasagna or stuffed shells," Aunt Tilde said. She was standing next to Mildred, sipping her coffee. "Who wants to spend all that time puttering around in the kitchen to make lasagna when Mario's makes a wonderful one?"

"Not to mention cleaning up afterward," Mildred said. "I don't blame Nora for going to Mario's. I would have, too."

"And why didn't you?" I asked, crossing my arms across my chest. "Instead of sending Nora to do your dirty work."

"Well, I didn't feel like Italian food," Mildred said as if it was the most obvious reason in the world. "And you haven't told us your news yet."

"How did you even know we were going to be at Mario's?" I asked, pointedly ignoring the question.

"I don't know what you're talking about," Mildred said. "I didn't have anything to do with it."

"Which is why Nora was taking notes," I said.

"I definitely had nothing to do with that," Mildred said with a grimace. "The woman never takes notes. I don't know why she was doing that yesterday."

I pointed at her. "Aha! You admit it. You did send Nora."

"I admit no such thing," Mildred said.

"It helps that the owner of Mario's was one of Mildred's students," Aunt Tilde said. Mildred glared at her.

Of course. I should have thought of it myself. Mildred was standing right there when Trisha asked us if we all wanted to go out for a double date, so all she needed to do was call around until she found our reservation. I was going to have to be a little sneakier in the future.

"And, to answer your question, no, I'm not pregnant," I said.

"Told you," Aunt Tilde said smugly.

Mildred shook her head in disgust and muttered something that sure sounded like "that will teach me not to send Nora to do anything."

Feeling vindicated, I picked up my coffee mug and settled into my chair as Mildred exasperatedly finished doctoring her coffee.

"Oh, you're needed today," Aunt Tilde said as she settled into her desk and began flipping through a stack of papers. "Scout, too."

I frowned as I looked up at her. Scout also lifted his head from his doggy pillow to do the same. "Needed for what?" I couldn't imagine what we were both needed for. Hopefully, Aunt Tilde hadn't signed us up for police dog training or something similar.

"Oh, nothing much," Aunt Tilde said, her forehead crinkling as she started skimming one of the papers. It appeared to be something photocopied, like part of an article or book. "Just some ghost hunting. No big deal."

I nearly spat out my coffee. "What? I thought we agreed you were going to focus on finding Hank the ghost while I tried to find out how he died. And why do you need Scout for ghost hunting?"

"Oh, that's right," Aunt Tilde murmured, only half-listening to me. "How is that going, by the way?"

"If you mean how finding out who killed Hank is going, I might have a lead," I said.

That got Aunt Tilde's attention. She lifted her head, blinking owlishly at me from behind her bright-orange glasses. "You might know what happened to Hank?" Her voice was eager, and I immediately felt rotten for overstating what I had discovered. Even Mildred had perked up and was looking at me, still stirring her coffee absentmindedly.

"Well, not exactly," I said, ducking my head so I didn't have to see the disappointment in their faces. "At least not yet. But I do have a lead." *Although not much of one,* I thought but didn't say. Instead, I gave them both a quick rundown of what MaryBeth had told me about Jazzy, her pimp, and The Dawn of Hope.

"So Jazzy was the one who killed Hank," Mildred said thoughtfully as she finally took a sip of her coffee and made a face. She reached for the coffeepot and started pouring more into her cup.

"I don't think it was Jazzy," I said, although I probably should have known that would be Mildred's takeaway. "MaryBeth didn't think there was anything going on between Hank and Jazzy."

Mildred waved a hand. "Oh, how would she know? She was the one who saw him buying her lunch, right?"

"Well, yes …"

"Then that settles it," Mildred said matter-of-factly.

"Just because he bought her lunch doesn't mean he was paying for sexual favors," I said.

Mildred shot me her exasperated look. "Why else would he be buying her lunch then?"

I threw up my hands. "Who knows? Maybe he was just being nice to her."

"Of course he was," Mildred said. "He wanted a better deal for his sexual favors."

"Emily might have a point," Aunt Tilde said before I could throw my hands up again. "Maybe he was trying to be nice."

"Oh, not you too," Mildred said.

"But you actually met Hank," Aunt Tilde said. "Did you ever think Hank, of all people, would be paying for prostitutes?"

"Of course not," Mildred said. "But that was before he was found murdered in a back alley with his pants down."

Aunt Tilde opened her mouth and then closed it with a snap. I shared her frustration, as even though I had never met Hank, it didn't seem like he was the type of guy to have been cheating on his wife with prostitutes. Especially the young and vulnerable ones.

But as much as I didn't want to believe it, I couldn't dismiss how he had died.

"What if it wasn't Jazzy who killed him, but her pimp?" I asked.

"Even if that were the case, it doesn't exonerate Hank from trying to stiff a prostitute," Mildred said before her cheeks turned pink after realizing what had come out of her mouth. "Pun not intended. But pimps don't kill johns who pay their bills."

Ugh. That was likely true, as well. I rubbed my temples, wishing I could think of another explanation, any other explanation, than Mildred being right.

"But I think it's good for you to go talk to Dawn of Hope," Aunt Tilde said. "Hopefully, they were able to get Jazzy off the streets, which is why she disappeared. And if you can locate her, maybe you can get some closure for Ruth."

"Yeah, I'll do that," I said, even as I pictured MaryBeth's doubtful face. Even if Jean hadn't retired and moved to Florida, I suspected I wouldn't find answers there. If Jazzy had gotten off the streets, and that was a big IF, it probably wasn't through The Dawn of Hope.

But what else was I going to do? It was a long shot, but I needed to keep digging. I owed it to Ruth to do whatever I could to find the answers.

"Just don't do it today," Aunt Tilde said. "Or at least, wait until after the ghost hunting."

Oh, the ghost hunting. I'd almost forgotten about it. "And why do I need to be there? And why am I bringing a dog?"

"Well, you know, ghosts." She gave me a conspiratorial look, as if ghosts were like celebrities, and you just had to deal with their strange whims.

"Are you saying a ghost asked for me to bring Scout?" I asked before another thought struck me. "And why did you say 'ghosts'? Does Ruth have more than one?"

"Heavens, I hope not," Aunt Tilde said. "She's having enough trouble keeping track of just one."

"And that one was her husband," Mildred said, her voice deadpan. "Imagine what would happen if they weren't related to her? Who knows what might be unleashed."

I ignored Mildred. "Then who wants to see Scout? Hank?"

"What? Emily, don't be silly." Aunt Tilde lowered her chin to look at me over her glasses. "If we had been able to contact Hank, why would we be ghost hunting?"

"Well, why does a dog have to be there?" Some days, I swear it felt like pulling teeth.

Aunt Tilde looked at me as if I were missing the obvious. "Well, to track Hank, of course."

I blinked at her as a ball of dread started to form in my stomach. This couldn't be good. "You want Scout to track Hank? How, exactly?"

"Well, by smelling him," Aunt Tilde said matter-of-factly, like a dog being able to track a ghost by smelling him should be an obvious plan.

"You think Scout will be able to smell Hank?"

"Why not? That's what dogs do, right?" Aunt Tilde asked. "They can find all sorts of things by smelling them. It's quite remarkable, when you think about it, how sophisticated a dog's nose is."

"Absolutely," Mildred said. "Just like how they sniff each other's butts, too."

"Those tracker dogs don't," Aunt Tilde said.

"Of course they do. All dogs do," Mildred said.

"Just so we're clear," I interrupted before the conversation got any more derailed. "You want me to bring Scout so he can track Hank by smelling him."

Aunt Tilde bobbed her head up and down. "Yes."

"Hank, the ghost," I said again.

"Well, we certainly don't need Scout to find Hank's body," Aunt Tilde said. "We know where that is. At least I hope he's still buried where he's supposed to be."

This had to be the most absurd plan. Not only that, but I couldn't believe I had to state the obvious. "But ghosts don't smell."

"Nor do they have butts," Mildred said, shooting Aunt Tilde a look. "I told you this was a silly idea."

"You don't need a butt for a dog to smell you," Aunt Tilde said. "Dogs smell things with no butts all the time. And besides, ghosts DO have butts. They were humans once."

"How many ghost butts have you seen?" Mildred demanded.

"How many just plain ghosts have *you* seen?" Aunt Tilde challenged right back, raising an eyebrow.

"So, regardless of whether ghosts have butts or not," I said, jumping in again before the conversation could devolve any further into ghost anatomy, "I don't think Scout is going to be able to track a ghost."

"We won't know, for sure, unless we let him try," Aunt Tilde said.

"While true in theory, in reality, I don't see how Scout can track a ghost when there is no smell to track."

"But ghosts DO have smells," Aunt Tilde said as she started waving the photocopied pages on her desk. "This article talks about it."

"Oh, well, if there's an article about it," Mildred said, rolling her eyes.

"And Ruth talked about how she could smell Hank. That's how she knew he was there," Aunt Tilde said, shooting Mildred a look.

"But that doesn't mean Scout is actually going to be able to track Hank using that smell," I said.

"You don't know that he won't," Aunt Tilde said as she started pawing through the stack of papers on her desk. "Dogs are very sensitive to paranormal activity. In fact, they're usually the first ones to sense the ghost. I have an article about this, as well."

"Is that what all of those papers are?" I asked, watching her rifle through the pages. "Articles you've photocopied?"

"How else am I going to research how to find a ghost?" Aunt Tilde asked, her voice muffled, as she had her head down searching through the piles.

"Do any of those articles talk about a ghost having a butt?" Mildred asked.

"While I've also heard that animals are more sensitive around psychic phenomena than humans," I interrupted again, "the whole reason we're hunting for a ghost is because Ruth claims the ghost left. If the ghost has left, then what exactly is there to track?"

Aunt Tilde stopped digging around and just sat there for a moment, head down, shoulders slumped. "Can't we at least try?"

I exchanged a glance with Mildred. "Well, sure. Of course we can try …"

"It's just, I'm not sure what else to do, if this doesn't work," Aunt Tilde interrupted.

"I keep saying, we should just do a seance," Mildred said. "Or maybe find a Ouija board."

Aunt Tilde shot her a look. "You know she won't do that."

"Why?" I asked. Not that I was a fan of either seances or Ouija boards, but I also didn't know any other methods for communicating with the spirit world.

"Because Hank always thought those things were a ridiculous waste of time," Aunt Tilde said.

"Was this before or after Hank became a ghost?" Mildred asked.

Aunt Tilde shook her head. "She says Hank would never have done either of those things when he was alive, and he sure won't be showing up now that he's dead. She also says she doesn't trust either of those methods. Said it's too easy to get conned, because you have no idea what ghost or spirit you're actually talking to."

"Oh, now she's worried about being conned," Mildred said. "It would have been nice if she had exercised a little of that discernment before she hired the gardener to do her accounting."

Aunt Tilde took off her orange glasses and rubbed her eyes. "Well, that basically means we don't have a lot of options to find her missing ghost, so if you won't bring Scout …" she let her voice trail off meaningfully before peeking at me with one eye.

Ugh. Like I was going to say no to that. Not that I would be able to refuse anyway. Aunt Tilde had a way of always getting what she wanted.

"Scout and I can try," I said with a sigh.

Aunt Tilde dropped her hands, put her glasses back on her nose, and clapped her hands. "Yes! Thank you. Ruth is going to be so pleased."

"Hopefully, she isn't expecting much," I warned. "I honestly don't think this is going to amount to much of anything."

Aunt Tilde simply beamed at me. "I'm sure it's all going to work out the way it's supposed to."

That's what I'm afraid of, I thought but didn't say. Instead, I forced a smile on my face and hoped for the best.

Chapter 14

Even though I knew, logically, that it wasn't a big deal to bring Scout to Ruth's house, I couldn't shake the niggling feeling that it was a bad idea. What did I think was going to happen? Scout would walk around, sniff a few things, and be done. Quick and painless.

However, the closer we got to Ruth's front door, the louder that niggling feeling became. It also matched the loud commotion that seemed to be going on inside Ruth's house.

"Heavens, what is that racket?" Aunt Tilde asked, cocking her head to one side at one particularly loud crash. "Is that Sally I hear?"

It took me a minute to remember that Sally was a cat, and not another person in this odd, unfolding saga.

"If it is Sally," Mildred said, frowning slightly at the loud yowl, "she sounds like she's scared to death. Maybe Hank finally came back."

"Or maybe a chipmunk got in again," Aunt Tilde said, her brows furrowing.

"Chipmunk?" I asked nervously, glancing uneasily at Scout, who had his ears perked as he stared at the front door. "I don't know if it's a good idea to have Scout here if there's a chipmunk loose inside."

"Why? Scout can catch the chipmunk and then locate Hank," Aunt Tilde said. "A two-for-one."

"You're assuming the chipmunk will go quietly," Mildred said. "I would say, based on the noise, that the chipmunk is probably winning."

The door suddenly burst open, and Ruth stood in front of us, looking completely disheveled. Her short-sleeve, blue, button-down shirt was untucked on one side and missing several buttons. There was also a rust-colored stain on it. Her black pants were covered with cat hair, and her own hair was flying every which way. "Oh my gosh, I'm so glad you're here. Come in, quick!" She reached over and grabbed Aunt Tilde to yank her inside, which was when I saw the scratch on her wrist. It looked deep—deep enough to have drawn blood.

The rest of us quickly followed them into the entryway, Scout straining at the leash. "Ruth, what is going on?" Aunt Tilde asked. "Did another chipmunk get in here?"

"I wish it were a chipmunk," Ruth said, pushing her hair out of her face. I could see that her eyes were wild. "It's Smoke."

Aunt Tilde blinked at her. "Smoke? You mean …"

"Oh look, they're playing," Nora's voice floated toward us from further in the house. Ruth turned pale and hurried away from us.

"You have got to be kidding me," Mildred muttered as we quickly followed.

The scene that greeted us was absolute chaos. The entire living room was in shambles. The loveseat, chair, and coffee table were on their sides, and the mail and various papers were spilled across the entire floor. The phone was off its hook, and I could hear it beeping. Two lamps were also lying on the floor.

In the middle of the mess was Smoke, and a second orange and white cat that I could only assume was Sally. They were hissing at each other, hair on end, as Nora fluttered nearby, wringing her hands together. As we watched, Smoke took another swipe at Sally, claws extended, and Sally let out another yelp. Scout was straining on his leash, and it was all I could do to hold him back.

"Nora, why on Earth did you bring Smoke?" Mildred asked, her voice dripping with disbelief.

Nora looked at her in surprise. "To help find Hank."

Mildred waved toward the two cats, who were still circling each other. "How is this helping Hank?"

"Well, cats are good at sensing any sort of supernatural phenomenon," Nora said. "And with Emily bringing Scout, I figured the more, the merrier."

"But there's already a cat here," Mildred said. "And if Sally wasn't able to find Hank, why would Smoke be able to?"

"Because Smoke is a trained investigator," Nora said with a sniff. "He knows how to do this."

Smoke let out another yowl, and again, his claw shot out at Sally, who hopped back a foot. At the same moment, my hands slipped, and I let go of the leash. Scout immediately bounded forward, skidding to a stop in front of Smoke, who immediately let out a shriek and fled to the corner of the living room, knocking over another lamp in the process, with Scout in hot pursuit. Sally, for her part, didn't waste a second and darted for the stairs, disappearing up them in a flash as Ruth plaintively called her name.

"Oh, look!" Nora said, "Smoke, your friend Scout is here!"

"I don't think they're friends," Mildred said. Scout had cornered Smoke in the corner. Smoke was bristling, but he wasn't making any move to attack Scout the way he had been doing with Sally.

"Oh, of course they are," Nora said. "They're dogs and cats. That's how they play."

"I'd better check on Sally," Ruth said worriedly. She was peering up the staircase as though she was going to find Sally hiding on one of the stairs.

"You should go do that," Aunt Tilde said. "And while you're up there, find something of Hank's for Scout to sniff."

Ruth brightened. "That's a great idea," she said as she started to climb the staircase.

"I don't know about this," I said to Aunt Tilde in a low voice. Scout hadn't taken his eyes off of Smoke, who looked like he really wanted to climb up the wall.

"Oh, they'll be fine," Nora said. "Just give them a few minutes to settle in, and then they'll both be ready to find Hank."

I couldn't imagine that either of them were going to be the slightest bit interested in ghost hunting after the current ordeal, but before I could figure out a more diplomatic answer, there was the sound of a door slamming from upstairs and Ruth came padding down, holding a comb in her hands.

"Here," she said, her face beaming. "I got something for Scout to smell." She thrust it at me, as if she expected me to take it.

I hesitated, staring at it, not sure whether I should touch it or not. Wouldn't that mess up Hank's scent? Although, honestly, how much of his scent could still be on there after ten years?

She shook it proudly in front of me. "See, it even has a few strands of his hair in it."

"Yeah, I can see that," I said, still not touching it. "But do you think after ten years, the scent would still be there?"

"Of course," Aunt Tilde answered, even though I couldn't see how she could possibly know that answer. "Smells are there forever. Plus, the hair is there, so the smells would still be there."

I was still skeptical, but Ruth was still waving the comb in front of me, expecting me to take it, so I finally did. After all, Ruth had been touching it, so either Hank's scent was going to be on there or it wasn't, and there wasn't much I could do either way.

I approached Scout, holding the comb. Scout gave it a couple of polite sniffs and then looked at me like he had absolutely no clue what he was supposed to do about it.

"I don't know," I said. "I'm not sure if this is working."

"Maybe he just needs a moment," Ruth said.

A moment to do what, I wanted to ask, but didn't.

"Let him sniff it again," Aunt Tilde urged.

"He probably needs to sniff something that Hank the ghost, touched," Mildred said. "After all, we're looking for a ghost, right? Not a human."

"But ghosts don't touch anything," Nora said. "What are we going to have him sniff?"

Ruth snapped her fingers. "Oh, I know. I've got the perfect thing." She hurried out of the room before any of us could say anything, and a moment later, she was back with the alphabet message board that had hung on the fridge. It still had the word "Bye" on it near the top, with the rest of the letters scattered haphazardly near the bottom.

"This should work," Ruth said, thrusting it toward Scout. "I haven't touched it since Hank left, so I'm sure Hank's scent would still be on it."

Scout gave Ruth a skeptical look but obediently bent to sniff the refrigerator magnets. I was expecting the same sort of reaction as when he sniffed the comb, but to my utter astonishment, his ears perked up, his body tensed, and he began sniffing the room.

"Oh my gosh, it worked," Aunt Tilde said, her tone as shocked as I felt, which made me think she hadn't believed it was going to work either.

"Well, he got the scent of something," Mildred said. "Although for the life of me, I can't see why Hank would have used his butt to move those refrigerator magnets."

Ruth looked at her in confusion. "His butt? Why would Hank use his butt to move letters on the refrigerator? He would just use his finger, right?"

Mildred started to explain the dog-smelling-butts theory when Scout put his nose to the floor and headed out of the room, tail wagging. I followed him as he circled the kitchen, pausing near the fridge, and then making a beeline straight into the laundry room.

"See? He DID get Hank's scent!" Aunt Tilde said from behind me, her voice triumphant.

"I guess so," I said. I couldn't even hide how floored I was. Scout was now standing in front of the back door, wagging his tail as he sniffed around the frame.

"See, he tracked him right to where he was going out. I told you this was going to work," Aunt Tilde said, sounding almost gleeful.

"I ... I don't know what to say," I said as I watched Scout sniff around the door. My mind was racing. Was it really possible that ghosts had a scent after all? And that Scout could actually smell it? It still seemed so far-fetched, yet I couldn't discount what my own eyes were showing me.

"You can say that you can find Hank," Aunt Tilde said.

My stomach seemed to plummet to the ground. Even if Scout could smell Hank, how would I possibly find him? "I don't know if that's possible," I said, watching as Scout moved from the door to the counter next to the door. "I doubt Scout is going to be able to pick up on Hank's trail once he's outside, and then what am I going to do?"

Aunt Tilde shook her head exasperatedly. "Stop being such a Debbie Doubter. You didn't think he was going to be able to pick up Hank's smell inside the house, either, and look at him now."

I had to admit she had a point.

"Maybe Hank didn't leave after all," Mildred said from behind us. I hadn't even realized she'd followed us into the laundry room. "Maybe he's over there." She pointed to the corner that Scout was furiously sniffing. "Or maybe that's where he used to sit a lot," she continued as Scout started frantically pawing at the floor, his claws scratching as they dug into the linoleum.

"Scout," I said, hurrying over to grab him by the collar. The last thing I wanted him to do was destroy Ruth's floor. "Stop that."

"Hank couldn't sit there," Aunt Tilde said. "It's too small. He would never be able to fit."

"How would you know? Have you seen a ghost?" Mildred asked as I managed to haul Scout far enough away that I could peer into the space between the counter and the wall.

"Do you see anything?" Aunt Tilde asked.

"I don't know," I said, squinting my eyes. "It's too dark. I need a flashlight." It seemed like there might be something there, but when I angled my head differently, it didn't look like anything changed.

Aunt Tilde turned. "Ruth, do you have a flashlight?" she started to call out, when she was interrupted by a loud yell, a bang, and a crash. In a flash, Scout had wriggled himself out of my grasp and went tearing off, his nails clicking on the tile floor. I heard Ruth shouting, but I couldn't make out the words.

"Oh dear," Aunt Tilde said, and the three of us hurried to the living room just in time to see Scout barrel into Smoke, rolling him into a small decorative table that, until that moment, had managed to avoid the rest of the chaos. The table went crashing to the floor, along with two glass figurines of dancing girls, exploding into fragments that scattered everywhere.

"Oh no, Scout," I called out, running over to pull him off the sputtering cat. "What have you done? Ruth, I'm so sorry."

Ruth was standing on the landing, wringing her hands while Sally peered out from behind her leg. Nora was on the stairway, her cheeks stained an unbecoming red.

"What's Sally doing down here?" Mildred asked.

"Oh … well …" Nora faltered. "I thought Sally might feel like she was missing out on all the fun, so I opened the door."

"Why would you do that?" Mildred asked, gesturing toward the broken glass, the tipped-over table, and the extremely angry cat.

Nora looked even more embarrassed. "I thought they were friends. They were just playing. I didn't expect them to get so ... rambunctious."

"We'll clean it up," Aunt Tilde said to Ruth, eyeing the mess before glaring at Nora, who flushed an even deeper red. "Nora, do you want to fetch a broom?"

Nora swallowed. "Of course," she murmured, hurrying down the stairs. "Ruth, I'm so sorry."

"It's okay. I'm more worried about someone or some pet stepping on the glass," Ruth said, still staring at the pile of glass shards.

"I'm happy to pay to replace whatever was broken," Nora said.

"No, that's not necessary," Ruth said. "I don't even think you can buy them anymore. They were gifts from my mother-in-law."

"Oh!" Nora covered her mouth with her hand, but doing so couldn't cover up how mortified she looked. "Ruth, I don't know what to say. I'm so very, very sorry."

Ruth blinked a couple of times and turned toward her. "Don't be. I always hated those little dancing girl statues, but I could never get rid of them, because Hank absolutely refused to hear a word against them. Even after my mother-in-law, God rest her soul, died. It was one of the few things we argued about. So in a way, you've done me a favor, just as long as no one gets cut on the glass."

"Oh, well ... in that case ... um, you're welcome?" Nora looked even more flummoxed than she had before.

"Emily, why don't you take Scout outside while we clean everything up?" Aunt Tilde asked. I nodded, as I was still holding onto Scout for dear life while he continued staring down Smoke, who was doing his best to ignore him.

"While you're out there, maybe let him sniff around and see if he can catch Hank's scent," Aunt Tilde added.

"Oh, that would be wonderful, if Scout could do that," Ruth said happily.

Great. Now I was going to be the one to disappoint Ruth. I glared at Aunt Tilde, but she just gave me an innocent smile in return. Ugh. I focused on getting the leash on Scout and wrestling him outside.

The moment Scout was on the grass, he loosened up, wagging his tail and looking at me with a happy grin as if to say, "See, mom? I did a good thing in there."

"Yeah, I don't know about that," I told him. He wagged his tail harder before getting distracted by a butterfly flying by.

"I don't suppose you can still smell Hank out here?" I asked him.

He looked at me, then started sniffing the ground. Seriously? Did he really … but then he picked up his leg, and I sighed.

Across the street, a middle-aged woman was watering geraniums in flowerpots. She had black hair streaked with gray, cut very short, oversized sunglasses, a large, pink tee shirt with a faded picture of a cat on it, and gray shorts. She hadn't seen me yet, as she was very focused on her watering, but I suddenly realized that she was in front of Lynne's house, the neighbor who supposedly looked in on Ruth. Could this be her?

I quickly tugged on the leash and headed across the street to introduce myself.

***

My luck held, as it was, indeed, Lynne. And she was happy to talk to me, once I identified myself as Tilde's niece.

"I haven't seen Tilde in ages," she said, putting down the watering can and running a hand through her hair, causing some of the strands to spike up. "How is she doing?"

"She's good," I said as Scout stretched his neck out to sniff her. "I know she'd love to see you. We tried coming over, but you were gone."

"Yes, my daughter just had her first baby. My first grandbaby." She smiled at the memory. "Her name is Missy, and she's absolutely adorable. I just got home an hour or so ago."

"You were there for a while?"

"A week." The smile disappeared from her face, and her eyes went to Ruth's house. "I would have loved to have stayed a little longer, but I didn't want to leave Ruth alone for so long."

126

"It's good she has you looking in on her," I said.

She pushed her sunglasses up on her nose. "I do what I can. I feel bad for her, all alone in that house. God forbid I ever find myself in that situation, I hope I have a neighbor looking out for me."

I shivered, even though the day was warm and the sun was shining. It felt almost like the old saying—that someone had walked across my grave. I gave myself a quick shake and sternly told myself to focus. "Yeah, I feel the same way. Speaking of looking out for Ruth, did you ever meet Bradley?"

Her face darkened. "Unfortunately, yes, I've met Bradley, or whatever his name is. Does this mean he's been hanging around again?"

"No, he hasn't been back." Did Lynne really say, "whatever his name is"?

"Good." She made a face as she fiddled more with her sunglasses. "I probably shouldn't say that, as I know Ruth likes him. But I think he was bad news."

"Why do you think that?"

She shrugged and looked back at Ruth's house. "Just a feeling. I don't have any proof of anything, other than he was a terrible gardener. I would come over and see him just standing around the yard, holding a pair of shears but not doing anything with them. When he'd see me, he'd quickly start chopping away at whatever was in front of him, even if it shouldn't be trimmed. He nearly killed a couple of her bushes that way." She shook her head. "I tried telling Ruth, but she refused to hear a word against him. I finally just had to let it go. I figured the worst thing that would happen is that her yard would be in terrible shape." She paused and focused on me. "Or is something else going on?"

I didn't want to tell her about the property tax fiasco—at least not yet. "What did you mean by 'whatever his name was'? Do you have any reason to believe his name isn't Bradley?"

Her mouth twisted as if she had eaten a lemon. "I was at the store one day, picking up a few things. I had just finished and was about to get into the checkout line when I saw Bradley. He was a few feet away, and his back was to me, but I still recognized him. He hadn't noticed me yet, and I wanted to keep it that way." She grimaced. "As you probably figured out, we aren't exactly friends. Anyway, as I was standing there with my cart, trying to figure out what to do—go back into one of the aisles or just stay where I was and hope he didn't turn around?—I heard this voice. 'Steven! Oh my gosh, I almost didn't recognize you.' I didn't think anything of it at first … until I realized the woman was speaking to Bradley."

"What did Bradley do?"

"He told her she had the wrong person; his name wasn't Steven. But she kept insisting it was. 'We went to school together! Don't you remember me? I'm Trina.' But he kept telling her she had the wrong person. I could tell he was getting more and more agitated, and finally, he told her that he had to go, and he walked out of the store. Just like that. Left his cart and everything. It was really bizarre."

"Did you ever ask Bradley about it?" I asked.

"He never saw me, so it didn't seem appropriate. And besides, it wasn't too long after that happened that he had to leave and help his 'family.'" The way she said the word "family" sounded like she was putting quotation marks around it. "I always wondered if it was because of what happened in the store with Trina."

"What about Ruth? Did you tell her?"

Lynne snorted. "Are you kidding? Of course I did. Did it make any difference? No. She still refused to believe anything bad about Saint Bradley. I don't know why she was loyal to him, but she was. I, for one, thought it was a blessing when he took off. The less he hung around her, the better." She cocked her head and studied me again. "Something else is up, isn't it? What is it? Please don't tell me Bradley was actually a con artist and stole all her money?"

I winced. "We're still trying to figure that out."

Her eyes widened, and she removed her sunglasses. "Oh no. What's going on?"

I gave her a brief rundown of the property tax situation, emphasizing that I didn't know much yet, but would hopefully find out more soon.

"Please keep me informed as well." She seemed really shaken. "I can't even imagine. If Ruth loses her home …" Her voice trailed off, and she shook her head. "Just please keep me updated."

I promised I would and hurried back across the street. Even though it still seemed like a long shot, I was hoping what Lynne just told me about Bradley/Steven would be enough to get to the bottom of the case. At least the property tax part of the case. The missing ghost part was a whole other issue.

Chapter 15

The Dawn of Hope operated out of a small office suite tucked away in a strip mall right off downtown Redemption. I parked the car, studying the sign that was posted on the glass door, which was simply a tasteful logo. There was no mention of what The Dawn of Hope did or even if it was open or closed. For an organization that was supposedly helping prostitutes get off the streets, it seemed to have a really low profile. I wondered how that was working out for them.

Not that it was any of my business. I wasn't there to help them with their operations, but to see if I could contact their past founder or find someone who was around ten years ago. I got out of the car and headed up to the door.

After I left Lynne, I immediately returned to Ruth's house to tell Mildred and Aunt Tilde about what Lynne had overheard at the grocery store. They were still in the middle of cleaning up, but at least Sally was back upstairs, and Smoke was sulking in the corner.

"His name is really Steven?" Mildred's eyes widened as she and Aunt Tilde exchanged a look. "That changes everything."

"Do you remember a Steven?" Aunt Tilde asked. "Or a Trina?"

"Wait, do you think Bradley was your student?" I asked.

"I thought it was at least worth checking," Mildred said. "But I couldn't find a Bradley. I found a few Brads, but one was married and living in another state, so I didn't think he fit. And a second unfortunately passed away a few years ago, so it couldn't be him, unless Bradley had found a way to come back from the dead …"

"Or was a zombie," Aunt Tilde piped in.

Mildred frowned. "Bradley couldn't be a zombie. He talks, and zombies don't talk."

"Do you remember a Steven?" I interrupted before the conversation went any further sideways.

Mildred furrowed her brow. "It's possible. I definitely had plenty of Steves, and one of them surely could have been a Steven. And Trina sounds familiar, as well. I'll go check my files as soon as we're done here."

"What about Hank?" Aunt Tilde asked. "Did Scout catch the scent?"

"Not yet," I said, and Aunt Tilde's face fell. I immediately felt bad—like I had disappointed her, even though I logically knew it would be impossible for Scout to locate a ghost. "I'll try again after I see The Dawn of Hope," I said, and Aunt Tilde perked up. I had no idea how that was going to work, but I would worry about it later.

Now, I pushed open the door to The Dawn of Hope and found myself in a small reception area covered with motivational posters. The furniture, two chairs and a couch, were worn out, and the scratched coffee table was covered with pamphlets.

"Hello? Can I help you?" A woman appeared in the doorway. She was older than me, maybe late forties or early fifties, with brown hair that was pulled back in a ponytail and large brown eyes. She wore loose jeans and a navy-blue tee shirt with a teddy bear on it. She gave me a warm smile, crinkling the skin around her eyes.

"Is this The Dawn of Hope?"

She nodded. "It is."

"I was hoping to speak to the person in charge."

"That would be me." She smiled again, holding out her hand. "I'm Carly."

"Emily," I said, moving forward to shake her hand. Now that I was closer, I saw she was probably younger than I had first thought, maybe late thirties or early forties. I could also see a faint scar on her neck that disappeared into her tee shirt.

"Welcome Emily. So how can I help you?"

"Actually, I was hoping you could help me locate the former person in charge. I think her name was Jean."

Her eyebrows went up in faint surprise. "That's a name I haven't heard in a while. She moved to Florida, I believe." She pursed her lips, tapping on her chin. "I'm not sure if I have a current phone number, but you're welcome to come into my office while I look."

"Thank you," I said, following her into a cramped room with a plain desk, several cheap wooden chairs, and rows and rows of metal filing cabinets. They lined every inch of wall space, crammed together as tightly as possible. It smelled musty, like it hadn't been properly cleaned in a while. She gestured for me to take a seat in one of the chairs across her desk while she went over to one of the filing cabinets and yanked open a drawer.

"If we have it, it should be here. But I will warn you, it's possible the file was either archived in storage or tossed. We did a massive overhaul this year and cleaned out a ton of old files. It was a huge job, but it needed to be done, as you can see. We don't have a lot of space." She waved her hand vaguely around the small room, and I agreed. "Can I ask why you want to get in touch with Jean?" Her voice was casual as she flipped through the files.

"I was hoping to talk to her about a prostitute she was helping. Well, who The Dawn of Hope was helping. This was about ten years ago. Her name was Jazzy."

Her fingers seemed to stumble on one of the files, but she quickly recovered. "Oh, well, I'm so sorry to disappoint you, but even if I could find Jean's number, she wouldn't be able to help. We take client confidentiality very seriously. It's the only way we can get our clients to trust us."

"Oh." It had never occurred to me a nonprofit would have a confidentiality clause, and I was thrown for a loop. "I guess that makes sense, but maybe you could make an exception in this case? It happened ten years ago."

Carly shook her head as she pushed in the drawer and came to sit down in front of me, folding her hands on her desk. "I'm sorry, but there are no exceptions. You have to understand. If word got out that we were sharing personal information, no one would trust us, and we would no longer be able to help get teenagers off the streets."

"I see," I murmured, even though I didn't. Wouldn't MaryBeth have known about the confidentiality policy if she had volunteered for them as long as she had? And if she had known, wouldn't she have told me about it when she handed over The Dawn of Hope's contact information? "Is this something new?"

She shook her head. "No, it's been the policy since I took over. Is there anything else I can help you with?"

Her tone, while still friendly, had noticeably cooled off, and there was a stiffness in her posture that hadn't been there a few minutes before. Her hands were empty, so I suspected I wasn't getting Jean's contact information. I probably also wasn't getting any contact information from anyone else who had been around ten years ago.

I forced a smile onto my face and stood up. "No, that won't be necessary. Thanks for your time."

***

The next morning, I was still puzzling over my strange conversation with Carly when Aunt Tilde and Mildred walked into the agency.

"Oh good, you're here and making coffee," Aunt Tilde said, balancing what appeared to be a large box of donuts on top of a stack of files. Mildred's arms were also filled with files. "Nick will be here shortly."

I froze, holding the coffee filter in one hand, a scoop of ground coffee in the other, my stomach immediately clenching. Nick was going to be here? Did I have enough time to run home and change into a nicer shirt and maybe style my hair and put on some makeup? No, that was overkill. It wasn't like we were dating or anything. I just needed to look … presentable. He was our attorney, and it was important to at least look professional if we were going to have a meeting. Hopefully, I would at least have some lipstick and mascara in my purse. Maybe I could take just a few minutes to fix my face before he arrived.

I hadn't seen Nick since that awkward double date. I was still mortified that Nora had been there, taking notes for heaven's sake. What must Nick think of me, I wondered? Would I ever be able to go on a regular date in this town? Maybe I needed to just throw in the towel and become a nun. I seemed to be incapable of having a normal relationship. But Jerome talked me off the ledge in his sweet, funny way, assuring me I was not to blame for my aunt's behavior nor any of her friends' behaviors. We were to have lunch later in the afternoon.

I also couldn't get Trisha's behavior out of my head. Why was she grilling Jerome about a date for her cousin? The whole thing still seemed so weird to me. And again, even though I knew I wasn't responsible for Trisha at all (it wasn't like we were friends or that I was even all that close with Nick), I still somehow *felt* responsible. If I hadn't been working at The Redemption Detective Agency, I never would have met Nick, which meant we never would have been on that double date to begin with. Again, Jerome told me I shouldn't blame myself, and while I appreciated that he seemed to be letting all the unfortunate dating fiascos roll off his back, I privately wondered how long that could last. I suspected he would eventually reach his limit with the craziness. How could he not? He was like me; he liked things neat and tidy and organized, with to-do lists and everything in its place. That used to be my life, but it certainly wasn't anymore. Why would he want to stick around in the messiness and chaos that was currently trailing after me like Pig-Pen's cloud of dirt in the old *Peanuts* cartoons? I wouldn't, if I were him.

"Emily?" Aunt Tilde was saying as she set down the donut box and the files, which promptly slid to the floor. Scout then walked over to them, so he could sniff the box. "Did you hear me?"

"Oh, yes," I said, even though I wasn't sure if I had heard it all. I quickly busied myself with the coffeemaker. "Nick is coming over."

"For a meeting," Aunt Tilde said, gently pushing Scout's nose away from the box. "He apparently has news."

"As do we," Mildred said triumphantly, setting down the files with a thump.

"And what's our news?" As soon as the words were out of my mouth, I inwardly braced myself for the answer. I had an awful feeling that I was going to somehow be part of the "news."

"I have an update on Bradley," Mildred said.

That perked me up. Maybe I wasn't going to be a part of it after all. "Oh? What is it?"

"You'll have to wait until Nick gets here," Mildred said mysteriously as she started organizing the files on her desk.

"Why can't you tell me now?"

Mildred shook her head. "Oh no. We have to keep this hush hush." She lowered her voice. "We can't have this information getting out."

"Why?" I asked in my normal tone of voice.

Mildred pointed at me. "That's why."

I stared at her. "What are you talking about?"

She dropped her voice again. "We can't have this information getting out. What if the newspaper gets wind of it? That could ruin everything."

"The newspaper? What are you talking about?"

Mildred shook her head firmly. "Nope. You're just going to have to wait until Nick gets here."

"We also have your news, Emily," Aunt Tilde said as I was opening my mouth to argue some more. "About being able to find Hank."

I closed my mouth with a snap. Ugh. That was exactly what I was afraid of. "I think it might be a stretch to say I'm going to find Hank."

Aunt Tilde flapped her hands. "Of course you're going to. Or, rather, Scout is. You saw him. He had Hank's scent. It's the only explanation."

"I agree he was smelling something," I said. "Whether or not it was Hank is debatable. And even if it was Hank, that doesn't mean Scout is going to be able to locate his scent outside."

"Have some faith. Scout has a great nose. Don't you, Scout?" Aunt Tilde said, looking down at Scout. Scout gazed back up at her and wagged his tail. "See? He knows what I'm talking about."

"I think he's really asking for a doughnut," I muttered as I poured myself a cup of coffee.

"I got your favorite," Aunt Tilde said, flipping open the box. "A cherry-filled Kringle."

Kringles were a Danish pastry and Wisconsin favorite, because they were amazing. Buttery and light and absolutely melted in your mouth. I moved closer to the box, feeling my mood improve. "When is our meeting with Nick?"

"Oh, not for a couple of hours," Aunt Tilde said as she pushed the box toward me with a little smile. "More than enough time to have a piece or two." She winked at me.

And enough time to slip into the bathroom once I was done eating it. It was almost enough to forgive her for the Hank the ghost nonsense.

Almost.

Chapter 16

"Bradley's real name is Steven Cunningham," Mildred announced once Nick arrived at the agency, his tie crooked and hair mussed up. He greeted us all with a smile, but it seemed a little forced. I almost felt queasy, which I wasn't sure was from eating too much Kringle, or because being around Nick always made my stomach twist up in knots. Except these knots didn't feel like I normally felt around Nick. These made me feel more ... uneasy.

"How can you be sure?" I asked, trying to ignore Nick and my uncomfortable feelings. He was leaning against the desk right next to mine, a cup of coffee in hand, having refused the pastry. I could practically smell his intoxicating scent of shampoo and soap mixed with his maleness. I gave my head a quick shake, trying to clear my thoughts.

Mildred gave me an exasperated look. "How many Stevens do you think were in my classes? Especially in the same class as a Trina."

"Trina also verified that she saw Steven Cunningham," Aunt Tilde said.

"So you talked to Trina?" Nick asked, taking a sip of his coffee.

"Yes. Although it was a little tricky to find her," Mildred said. "She's married now, so she changed her name."

"How did you find her?" I asked.

"Called her parents," Mildred said. "They, on the other hand, were easy to find, as they're still in the same house and have the same phone number as they did when Trina was in my classroom. They gave me Trina's new name and number, and Voila."

I had to admit, that was better sleuthing than I expected from Mildred.

"Did Trina remember seeing Bradley, or Steven, at the grocery store?" Nick asked.

"Oh, did she ever," Mildred said as she gestured wildly with her hands. "She couldn't figure out why Steven would lie about knowing her. She asked me if I knew of any reason, but I of course didn't say anything." She had a smug look on her face, almost like butter wouldn't melt in her mouth.

"Then how did you answer her?" I asked.

"I told her it was probably because of his upbringing. He was probably embarrassed about his family," Mildred said. Now, her expression was more like the cat who ate the canary. She folded her hands on her desk and looked at both of us.

Nick and I exchanged a glance. He was the one who decided to bite. "Upbringing?"

Mildred leaned across the desk, her eyes gleaming, as if she had been dying for one of us to ask. "It was really a sad situation. The year he was in my classroom, his parents were in the middle of a nasty divorce. I know he was spending some of his time with his grandparents because his parents were fighting so much."

"Oh, that's really kind of heartbreaking," I said. I could almost feel sorry for him … if he hadn't just conned poor Ruth out of her house.

"It actually was," Mildred said. "He was such a sad kid. He didn't misbehave much, mostly just kept to himself. As you can imagine, his grades were terrible. I was afraid I was going to have to hold him back a year, but his mother came in and talked me out of it. She promised she would hire a tutor for him over the summer and get him caught up before the next school year started."

"Did she?" I asked.

"I actually don't know," Mildred said. "She moved out of Redemption that summer and took Steven with her."

"What about the husband?" Nick asked.

"He stayed here. At least, that's what I heard at the time."

"Did Steven ever come back?" Nick asked.

"You mean before becoming Ruth's accountant-gardener? I don't know. If he did, I didn't hear about it," Mildred said.

This was getting stranger and stranger. "I wonder why he would come back now," I said. "Although didn't Ruth say he worked with Hank, and that's why he wanted to help her out?"

Mildred snorted. "I doubt he worked with Hank. He would have been, what—eighteen? Maybe nineteen—when Hank died?"

"Then what would the connection have been?" I asked. "Why would Steven have returned to Redemption to target Ruth?"

"Probably because he's a con artist," Mildred said. "Just like his dad."

"His dad was a con artist?" I asked.

"I'm sure of it," Mildred said.

"How can you be so sure?" I asked.

She looked at me as if it were obvious. "Because Steven had to learn it from somewhere."

I opened my mouth, closed it, and then decided to move on. "Okay, well even if he was a con artist, why would he pick Ruth? It's not like she had a lot of money. If he were really a con man, wouldn't he find a wealthier target?"

Mildred sighed. "Look, I like Ruth. I really do. But I think we can all agree she's not the brightest bulb. He probably thought she would be easy prey."

Nothing about this case was making sense. "But again, how would he even know Ruth?" I persisted. "Or Hank, for that matter."

"If I had to guess, I would say his dad probably knew Hank," Mildred said.

I stared at Mildred. I hadn't thought of that.

"Why would you say that?" Nick asked.

"Because he was just like Hank," Mildred said, flapping her hands.

Nick tilted his head. "How so?"

Mildred glared at him. "Oh, come on. You know exactly what I'm talking about. I shouldn't have to spell it out for you."

Nick folded his arms across his chest. "Pretend that I don't. How would you spell it out for me?"

Mildred threw up her hands. "Oh, for heaven's sake. His dad was a cheater. Just like Hank."

"Wait. Steven's dad was having an affair?" I asked.

"Why do you think his parents got divorced?" Mildred countered, as if it were the most obvious reason in the world.

"Yes, but Hank was … allegedly paying prostitutes. Was that what Steven's dad was doing, as well?" I asked.

"I have no idea, but a cheater is a cheater," Mildred said firmly. "If you ask me, Hank and Steven's dad were probably both paying that one prostitute … what was her name? The one who disappeared?"

"Jazzy," I said.

"Right. Jazzy. They were both her johns, and one day, they decided to kill her, and that's why she disappeared," Mildred said.

I stared at Mildred. "Um … but Hank was the one who was killed. Remember?"

Mildred waved her hand. "Hank was probably killed by accident."

My eyes widened. "By accident? He was stabbed and his pants were down around his ankles."

"Oh, that's right." Mildred frowned as she puzzled over it for a moment. "Okay, so maybe it was Jazzy and Steven's dad who killed Hank, and then they both had to disappear."

"Did Steven's dad disappear?"

"Well, I don't know where he is," Mildred said. "Do *you* know where he is?"

"No, of course not," I said.

"See," Mildred said, as if that answered the question. "Ergo, he's missing. Just like Jazzy. And that's why Steven decided to target Ruth. For revenge."

"But if that's what happened, why would Steven's son go out of his way to con Ruth?" I asked. "Hank would be the victim in all of this, right? What you're saying would make more sense if Steven's dad was the one who was found dead."

"True," Mildred said, tapping her chin. "So maybe it wasn't Hank who was killed, but Steven's dad."

"Of course it was Hank," Aunt Tilde said. "We all know it was Hank."

"But how do we all know? Who told us? Did any of us see the body?" Mildred asked.

"I'm sure we saw the body. We were at the funeral," Aunt Tilde said.

"No, it was a closed casket," Mildred said. "Remember, I even talked about it at the time. I thought it was really strange, that it was closed. And maybe we have our answer, because it wasn't Hank after all."

"I'm sure it was Hank," Aunt Tilde said, but she didn't sound as sure as she had. "If it wasn't Hank, then where has he been all this time?"

"Probably with Jazzy," Mildred said. "They probably ran off together. We need to dig up Hank's body in the graveyard, so we can verify if it was really him or not."

"That would require a court order, and I seriously doubt any judge would sign off on that," Nick said.

"The judge would, if he were interested in finding out the truth," Mildred said.

"If it wasn't Hank, then who was the ghost living with Ruth?" Aunt Tilde asked.

"Steven's dad," Mildred said. "If there even was a ghost, which I'm still not convinced. He's probably haunting her for revenge, which explains why he ran off after his son disappeared."

"So, we're making a lot of assumptions that may or may not be true," Nick smoothly broke in. "For instance, it's very possible that there is no link between Steven and Hank at all, and Steven just used Hank's name as a way to get close to Ruth."

"Then why would he pick Ruth?" I asked.

Nick looked pained. "I hate to say it, but Mildred is right that Ruth would have been a vulnerable target. And these con artists, they're like predators. They have a sixth sense when it comes to detecting weakness. It could have been as simple as what Mildred first said—that Steven was looking for an easy target and found Ruth."

"But Ruth will be okay now, right?" Aunt Tilde asked, her eyes full of hope as she stared at Nick. "We know who Bradley is now, and we know he conned Ruth ... so her house will be saved, right?"

Nick hesitated, and in that hesitation, I just knew whatever he was going to say was going to be bad.

Aunt Tilde knew it, too, because her face crumpled.

"I'm so sorry, Tilde," he said gently. "Unfortunately, it's not that simple."

"But he conned her," Aunt Tilde said. "It wasn't her fault."

"I know that. And believe me, I'll be arguing that, but …" he hesitated again. "Look, I'm going to try to get another extension before the state forecloses on her property, and it's possible they'll grant it. But even if they do, Ruth is still going to have to find some way to pay the back taxes, and right now, she's completely broke."

"Then we just need to get it from Steven," Aunt Tilde said.

"Yes, that would be ideal," Nick said. "Assuming he still has the money and hasn't spent it. But even if does have it, that doesn't mean Ruth gets paid back. He's going to have to go through the court system and be found guilty before she can petition the court to get her money back. And before the courts grant her petition, there will be appeals, and …" his voice trailed off, and he took a breath. "It's likely going to take years before it gets settled. And I don't think the state of Wisconsin is going to wait years to get its back taxes paid."

"Oh, no," Aunt Tilde said, covering her face with her hands. "Poor Ruth."

"Yeah," Nick said, his voice soft before straightening up. "But that's the bad news. The good news is that we have Bradley's real name, which means the cops can find and arrest him. That will help me convince the state of Wisconsin to grant Ruth an extension. It's also possible I could even get her tax bill reduced. And after that, we can explore other ways for Ruth to raise the money. But the first step is to open an investigation with the cops."

"Great! Let's go," Aunt Tilde said, standing up. "Mildred, I'll drive us to the police station."

"Actually, you'll need to go pick up Ruth first," Nick said. "She's the one who is going to have to file a report, as she's the victim."

"I can't do it?" Aunt Tilde asked.

"Unless Steven stole money from you as well," Nick said, then narrowed his eyes as he gave her a hard look. "*Did* Steven steal money from you?"

Aunt Tilde considered it. "Well …"

"Oh, for heaven's sake," I jumped in. "Aunt Tilde, you can't file a fake police report. That's a crime."

"Yes, but it is possible Steven stole from me," Aunt Tilde said. "There was that shady cable guy who showed up at the house once. Do you remember, Mildred?"

"Oh yes," Mildred said, bobbing her head. "You said after he left, there was a hundred dollars missing from your dresser."

"No, it was closer to two hundred," Aunt Tilde said.

"You know the same shady cable guy stole money from my house, too," Mildred said.

"Enough," I interrupted before Mildred and Aunt Tilde suddenly decided this shady cable guy had also stolen money from me. "Aunt Tilde, this isn't going to work. Go talk to Ruth. I'm sure once you and Mildred tell her who Steven, or I guess Bradley, really is, she'll want to report him."

Aunt Tilde sighed. "I don't think it's going to be that easy. I've been bringing up Bradley, err Steven, trying to warm her up to the idea he's a con artist, and she flat out refuses to hear a word against him."

"You really need to try to convince her," Nick said. "Because if you don't, it's going to be so much harder to convince the state that she was a victim."

Aunt Tilde grimaced. "Can you still get her an extension?"

Nick held up his hands. "I'll do whatever I can. But if she doesn't file a report, it's going to make my job more difficult." He flashed one of his charming grins, but it seemed a little duller than normal. "Not that I have ever backed down from a challenge." His eyes shifted to me, and I felt something twist in my stomach, although it could have been the Kringle. Our gazes held, maybe a beat too long, before I looked away.

Aunt Tilde kissed him on the cheek. "Thank you, Nick. We'll do our best. And hopefully, if Emily has any luck, we'll locate Hank, and he can help convince her."

I tried not to groan as Nick grinned again, except this time, it seemed more natural. "Really? Emily is on ghost-hunting duty?"

"Assuming it's really Hank's ghost haunting Ruth," Mildred said. "If it turns out to be Steven's dad, we may have a real problem on our hands."

"I'm not hunting ghosts," I said. "Not exactly."

Aunt Tilde flapped her hands. "Oh, don't be so modest. Of course you are. Scout is your dog."

Nick raised an eyebrow. "Scout is involved too?" At the sound of his name, Scout stopped snoring and lifted his head from his pillow while wagging his tail.

"Scout caught the smell of … something in Ruth's house," I said. "Whether it was a ghost or not is up for debate."

"Of course it was Hank," Aunt Tilde said. "Who else uses that little alphabet message board besides him?"

"Or rubs their butt against it," Mildred added.

"Wait? What?" Nick asked.

"Don't ask," I said.

"So now that Scout knows Hank's scent, Emily is going to see if Scout can track him," Aunt Tilde said.

"I would like to see that," Nick said, a gleam in his eye.

"I don't think there will be much to see," I said. "And yes, I will be taking Scout back to Ruth's house this afternoon," I hastily added, as I could see Aunt Tilde was just about to tell me again to do that.

"You're going to make Ruth so happy," Aunt Tilde said, clapping her hands.

I refrained from saying only if I actually found Hank, which was doubtful. And I had absolutely no idea what I was going to tell Ruth when I wasn't able to find her husband's ghost. "I'll do my best."

Scout looked up again with a doggy smile on his face as his tail thumped on the pillow. At least someone was looking forward to ghost hunting.

Chapter 17

Jerome was late for lunch, which was unlike him. Usually, he was early, as he subscribed to the belief that, when you arrive on time, you're late.

I was already seated at Aunt May's Diner. I had been lucky enough to score a booth in the corner. Located in downtown Redemption, Aunt May's was a popular breakfast and lunch spot, and it usually drew a respectable dinner crowd.

I worried the paper my straw came in between my fingers, turning it into a tiny ball before stirring my Diet Coke and glancing over at the clock again. Yes, he was definitely five minutes late.

Unless I had gotten the time wrong. I thought back over our conversation. No, I was sure he said one fifteen. He liked to have lunch a bit later to avoid the big rush.

So why wasn't he here?

I played with my straw, trying to tap down the uneasy feeling that was slowly uncoiling itself in my gut. Had he had enough of me and my crazy aunt, along with her equally nutty friends? Is that why we were having lunch in a restaurant rather than dinner somewhere, so I couldn't make a scene? Not that I would. I would feel bad, of course, but I couldn't really blame him. If I were him, I didn't know if I would take on my baggage either.

But the more I thought about him breaking up with me, the more I realized how much I had been looking forward to this lunch. I really wanted someone to talk to, someone who wasn't a part of the investigation. There was so much going on—trying to find a ghost, Bradley/Steven, Ruth likely losing her house. And I hadn't even had a chance to fully digest what had happened with The Dawn of Hope. I was sure Carly was hiding something, or at least not telling me the whole truth, but why would she do that? And how could I possibly find out what it was? I was going to have to do something. At the moment, I was pretty much at a dead end, no pun intended, investigating Hank's murder.

I really wanted someone I could talk to … someone who could maybe see something I missed. But Aunt Tilde was out. She had made it clear she wanted all my attention focused on finding Hank's ghost. Like that was going to happen. In her defense, I know she was really worried about Ruth losing her house, and I think she thought if we could at least bring some closure around the ghost, that would help Ruth. Mildred was … well, who knows what direction she would end up taking me. Same with Nora. And Nick was busy trying to save Ruth's house. Plus, it wasn't like we were friends or anything, so it probably wouldn't be appropriate to talk to him. Never mind he had always been a good sounding board, at least with our other cases …

"Sorry I'm late," Jerome said, sliding into the booth in front of me. His cheeks were flushed, as if he had been running, but otherwise, he was his normal pressed and tidy self with his hair carefully styled and button-down shirt pressed.

Actually, that wasn't exactly true. There was something different about him that I couldn't quite put my finger on. It was like he was excited or hyped up about something. I could practically feel him buzzing in anticipation, which only made me more concerned. Could he be that excited to break up with me?

I moved my hands to my lap so he wouldn't see me twisting my fingers around. "Did something happen to cause you to be late? Because you're usually so prompt," I hastened to add as I didn't want him to think I was nagging him.

His expression dimmed. "I know. I'm so sorry. You know how much I hate being late, but I promise you, it was worth it." That buzzing excitement was bubbling up again, and I could see him fighting to keep from smiling.

I squeezed my hands together. "So what is it?"

The waitress arrived at that moment to take our order, but neither of us had looked at the menu. He knew what he wanted—a turkey sandwich with coleslaw instead of fries. I ordered the same, as I didn't think it mattered what I got … I likely wasn't going to be able to choke down a single bite.

As soon as the waitress left, he started digging around in his briefcase. "I was going to wait until after we ate, but this is too good not to tell you."

I craned my neck slightly, trying to see what was in his briefcase. For the life of me, I couldn't figure out what he was going to show me. It wasn't like we were married, so it couldn't possibly be divorce papers. Maybe it was a restraining order against Aunt Tilde, Mildred, and Nora.

He pulled out a bundle of mimeographed papers, stapled together, and handed them to me with a flourish. I stared at the first page, unable to comprehend what I was seeing.

"This is ... is this a job application?"

"For school secretary," he said proudly. "It just opened up a day ago. I was waiting to get the paperwork, so I could bring it to you."

I skimmed over the job description, which included the starting salary ...quite a bit less than I was making when I worked for the Duckworths. Although, to be fair, it was a lot higher than I was making now, but as I also had very few bills, that hadn't been a problem yet. "I don't understand."

He leaned across the table. "It's a job. For you."

"A job?" I looked down again, trying to collect my scattered thoughts—I had been so sure he was going to break up with me— and found myself staring at the duties. "But I'm not a secretary."

He waved a hand. "Office manager. Whatever. It's basically a secretary."

I felt myself bristle. "Office manager and secretary are two very different jobs."

He gave me a look. "Are you going to tell me what you do for your aunt is much different from being a secretary?"

"Yes, it is different. Sure, I do some secretarial stuff, because it's a small business, but I'm actually running the operations. Which is also what I did when I worked for the Duckworths ... actually ran their operations."

He held up a hand. "Okay, look. I'm not trying to start a fight or offend you. I figured you could do the job of school secretary in your sleep, and obviously, you can. So, what do you think?

I was still trying to get my head around what was happening. "But I have a job."

He rolled his eyes. "You're helping your aunt and all her friends with her retirement hobby. I don't know what that is, but it's certainly not a job."

My back started to stiffen. "That's not true. The Redemption Detective Agency is an actual business."

He raised an eyebrow. "How many paying cases have you had?"

Not nearly enough. "This is still a brand-new business. Establishing yourself takes time."

"That may be true if they were serious about establishing themselves as a business. You seem to think they aren't."

Ugh. I had complained about that before. But I couldn't believe he was throwing it back in my face. "They're learning. It's not easy running a business. Or becoming a detective. They all worked for someone else doing something very different for most of their lives. Well, except for Nora, who probably should understand what it means to own a business, but that's neither here nor there …"

"No, it's not," Jerome said. "That's precisely my point. All of them are a mess. All of them. And you have no choice but to deal with them, because you're there with them all day. But if you had a different job, all of that changes. Don't you want your life back?"

I opened my mouth, then shut it again because I couldn't figure out what I wanted to say. One part of me wanted to say, "Of course, yes, I want my life back. Where do I sign?"

But another part of me, a deeper one, wanted to say, "I have a life, thank you very much."

Was that true? Living with my aunt, working for my aunt, being constantly involved with all my aunt's crazy schemes, not to mention her nutty friends, to the point where they followed me on my dates. Was that the life I really wanted?

But if I got a job, an actual job, all of that changed. I could move out … well, maybe. I'd have to see what Redemption rentals were like, because the salary was pretty low. But I would at least be able to pay Aunt Tilde rent. She had refused to accept any money from me so far, but if I found myself a job, it would be the least I could do.

I would finally have my own life, rather than being tied to whoever wandered into the agency on any given day.

Although … the faces of the people we had helped flashed through my mind. Sure, not all of them had paid. But still, we had helped them when others couldn't or wouldn't. And wasn't that worth something? I thought about Ruth. Maybe we wouldn't be able to save her house, but at least we were giving her a fighting chance—something she wouldn't have without us.

Jerome was sitting back in his chair, his arms folded across his chest as he studied me. "Emily, I don't understand you. I thought you'd be jumping for joy at this opportunity. It's not like you won't ever see your aunt or Mildred or Nora, but you'll be free of them. *We'll* be free of them. Don't you want that for us?"

Did I?

If Jerome had handed me this application the day I moved to Redemption, fresh off the bus, I would have jumped at it. But now?

"Not to mention you won't have to do any more investigating ever again." He rolled his eyes again. "We'd never have to talk about one of your cases again, either."

Everything about this current case I so wanted to talk about with him seemed to turn into a lump inside my throat. "You don't like hearing about my cases?"

He must have heard something in my voice because he uncrossed his arms and leaned forward. "Oh, come on, Emily. I didn't mean it like that. Of course I like hearing about your cases. But when you go on and on about them … I mean, I get it. It's frustrating when you don't have the resources to be able to solve them, which again, is part of the problem with working for a hobby instead of an actual business. If you were working for a real private investigator, I'm sure it would be very different, and it would be more fun to talk about your cases, instead of just listening to … how frustrated you are."

Was that how I sounded to him? Frustrated with solving cases?

Was that because I was frustrated?

The waitress arrived with our food, and I used the distraction as an excuse to tuck the application in my purse, deciding I would think about it later. Maybe after I took Scout back to Ruth's house to see if he could track her husband's ghost.

Ugh. Maybe I should take a closer look at the school secretary job after all.

***

When I returned from lunch, the door to The Redemption Detective Agency was locked, and the cheery sign that stated, "We're out Solving the Unsolvable, but don't you fret! We'll be back in no time flat. All you have to do is call us and leave a message, and we'll get right back to you" was attached to the door. Mildred and Aunt Tilde must have gone to a late lunch; or maybe, they were with Ruth trying to convince her to file charges against Bradley/Steven. As I unlocked the door, the sign fell off, but I left it where it was on the floor. I could reattach it to the door once I left with Scout.

Scout immediately got up and padded over to greet me. I buried my face in his soft fur as I hugged him. He felt so solid, so grounded. I wished I could stay like that forever.

Jerome had done most of the talking while we ate our sandwiches. Well, while he ate his sandwich. I mostly picked at mine. He told me all about the secretarial job and what I could expect, as though I had already been hired. When I reminded him I hadn't gone through the application process, much less had an interview, he waved it off like it was a minor detail. In other words, if I wanted the job, it was mine. I wasn't sure how legal that would be, him being the principal and me being his girlfriend, but he didn't seem that concerned about it, so I figured maybe I shouldn't be either.

The only thing I had to figure out was, did I want the job or not?

And as of that moment, I didn't have a clue.

While yes, there was no question The Redemption Detective Agency drove me nuts, and it would be nice not to have three elderly women nosing about in my business, I also wasn't sure if a job as a school secretary would be much better. Yes, I would be back to having an actual job, and as Jerome pointed out, even though I was overqualified for it, it would look good on my resume. Or at least better than working at The Redemption Detective Agency. I wouldn't need to stay forever—just long enough for the Duckworths to remove me from the blacklist, which hopefully, would only take a year or two. And then I could get a real job.

I could get my life back.

And wasn't that what I wanted more than anything?

I stood up, brushing my hands against my khaki shorts. What on Earth was wrong with me? Of course I wanted my life back. Why would I even consider anything else? Here I was in what used to be the dining area of a bankrupt restaurant to collect my dog to see if he could track a ghost.

Why would me leaving even be a question?

I headed over to my desk to stuff the application into one of the drawers. I would deal with it later. Right now, I needed to go find a ghost.

Scout had followed me over to my desk and was looking up at me, his eyes full of trust and love. I felt something twist inside me, although it made no sense. Instead, I bent down to pet him again and then reached for the leash to attach it to his collar.

The bell at the top of the door tinkled, and I looked up to see Nick standing there, looking more disheveled than normal, even more so than earlier that morning. His tie was loosened, the top button of his shirt was unbuttoned, and his eyes were exhausted.

"Oh, is Tilde here?" He ran a hand through his hair, messing it up more than normal, and I felt that twist inside me again.

"Sorry. I'm not sure where she is."

He nodded, but he appeared a little distracted. "Okay, I guess I'll track her down later." Scout was pulling at the leash, wanting to go greet Nick, which seemed to get his attention. "Going ghost hunting, I presume?"

"Don't even get me started," I muttered, reaching down to unclasp the leash. Scout bounded over to Nick as if he hadn't seen him in years rather than just a few hours.

He chuckled under his breath as he reached down to pet Scout. "I know it seems silly, and it is. But you are doing a good thing. So, try to keep that in mind." He glanced up and must have seen something on my face. "What's going on?"

"Nothing," I said, because it should be nothing. There was no reason why I should feel like crying. No reason at all. "But quite honestly, I don't see how any of this is good. All I'm doing is feeding a poor old woman's delusion that her husband's ghost has been with her for the past decade, when really, I should be focusing on saving her house."

"The property tax fiasco is my problem," Nick said easily. "Your aunt's job is to get Ruth to file a police report on Steven. And this is your job. Giving an old woman peace around her husband's death."

I threw my hands up. "But how can I give her any peace? I'm not going to be able to find a ghost for her. Instead, I'm going to end up being the bad guy having to tell her that I have no idea where her husband's ghost is."

"Don't be so sure of that," Nick said, flashing one of his trademark grins that always made my knees weak. "You might surprise yourself, or I guess I should say, Scout might surprise you. You could end up finding Hank after all."

I rolled my eyes. "Be serious."

"I am serious." His grin faded as he studied me. "You'll figure out what to say. You always do."

That lump grew in the back of my throat again, and I tried to swallow it down. "How can you be so sure?"

"Because you're good at this." He cocked his head and gave me a peculiar look. "You know that, right? You have a real knack for this."

I looked away quickly, blinking my eyes. My chest was so tight I could barely breathe. I couldn't figure out why I was so emotional. Maybe Jerome was right, and this job really was a bad influence on me.

"Emily?" Nick's voice was concerned. "What's going on?"

The gentleness in his voice was very nearly my undoing. I took a step back, breathing in deeply, as I struggled to pull myself together. "Nothing."

"It's not nothing. What's going on?"

I scrubbed at my face as I shook my head. "It is nothing. It's just … Jerome offered me a job today."

"Jerome did?" His voice became several degrees cooler. "I didn't realize principals could offer jobs like that."

"Well, I'd have to apply. But it's for a school secretary. I'm over-qualified for it, but still, it would be a solid job to have on my resume, for when I'm able to start applying for COO positions again."

"I see." Nick's voice was clipped. "That's why he offered it? Because it would look good on your resume?"

I looked down at my hands. "Well, he knows how much I want to get my life back. And he's not sure this private investigation thing is really ... a good use of my talents."

I couldn't even look at Nick, and I wasn't sure why. There was a long silence. "It sounds like you have a big decision to make. I'll get out of your hair."

"Nick," I said, even though I wasn't sure what to say or why I was even calling him back.

He paused, one hand on the door, and glanced back at me. His expression was flat, but it softened slightly. "I get why he would think this is a waste of time and talent. But I don't know if I would ever bet against your aunt once she's made up her mind about something. And it sure seems to me she's made up her mind to make this a success. Just think about it." A faint smile touched his lips, and then he was gone. "Good luck with your ghost hunting," he called out as the door swung shut.

Ugh. That man was so frustrating. He always knew just how to get under my skin.

The Mysterious Case of the Missing Ghost

Chapter 18

"Emily, Emily!"

Lynne was running across her yard, waving frantically at me as I completed my third lap around Ruth's house with Scout. Needless to say, while Scout was having a grand ole time strolling around in the fresh air and sniffing everything in sight, as far as I could tell, he had not caught the scent of any ghostly beings.

Not that I was terribly surprised.

And despite Nick's words floating through my head—how he was confident I would figure it out, and that I had a knack for this—all I could feel was a growing sense of panic that I was about to break Ruth's heart. As if losing her house wasn't enough; now, I was going to have to tell her that we had no idea how to locate her husband's missing ghost.

I definitely should take the school secretary job.

"Emily, you got a second?" Lynne asked, breathing hard as she caught up to me. Her black hair was sticking straight up, and her cheeks were red.

"Sure," I said. Anything to distract me from my own bleak thoughts.

"I wanted to know if you have any sort of update yet."

Ugh. Not really much of a distraction. "Unfortunately, no." I didn't feel like it was my place to share what Nick had told us earlier. At least, not until I had something solid. Right now, it was more of a laundry list of bad and more bad.

Lynne chewed on her lower lip and turned away, looking over my shoulder toward Ruth's house. "I'm just so worried about her. I don't know what to do."

"I know the feeling."

Her eyes shifted toward me, and I could see the understanding there. "I stopped in to see her yesterday, and ... well, you probably already know this, but she's really not herself. I haven't seen her this stressed and anxious for years … probably not since those first few terrible weeks after Hank died. I just have no idea how to help her."

I didn't know what to say. I wasn't sure if there was anything to say. At this point, we were both just spectators, unable to do anything to truly help as Ruth had her life ripped away. All because a horrible person decided to take advantage of a kind, naïve, trusting old woman.

After a moment, she looked down at Scout, who was busy nosing her hand. "Hi there, handsome, how are you doing?" She started stroking his fur as Scout gave her hand a friendly lick. "So, what are you doing with him? I saw you circle the house a couple of times."

I sighed. There didn't seem to be much use in hiding it. As Ruth's neighbor, I was sure she knew about Hank. "I'm actually looking for Hank."

Her hand stilled on Scout's fur, and she looked up at me, her expression puzzled. "Hank? You mean Ruth's Hank?"

"Well, technically, Hank's ghost." I was a little surprised by her reaction. Maybe Ruth forgot to tell her Hank had gone missing.

Lynne's brow furrowed. "Why are you looking for Hank's ghost?"

I explained how Ruth thought Hank had left. "She heard the back door slam, and when she went to check, she discovered that Hank had left the word 'bye' on the refrigerator magnet board."

By the time I was done talking, Lynne's jaw had dropped open. "Wait a minute. Ruth thinks Hank wrote those little notes on the refrigerator magnet board?"

I gave her a funny look. "Well, yeah. Who else would be?"

"Me."

I stared at her. "You? You were the one writing those notes?"

"Of course it was me. She couldn't possibly think that her husband's ghost was moving those magnets around."

"Um …" I wasn't sure what to say to that.

Lynne looked at me in disbelief. "Seriously? She really thought it was Hank?"

"Yes, she thought Hank had returned to her as a ghost and was living in the house with her." I tilted my head to study her. "You didn't know that?"

"I thought it was a joke," Lynne said. "I assumed she knew there was no such thing as ghosts, so it was just a fun joke to play to pretend Hank was still hanging around the house as a ghost."

I couldn't believe what I was hearing. All these years, Hank's ghost was actually the next-door neighbor? "Why did you write 'bye'?"

"Because I was about to leave to see my daughter for a week and I wanted to make sure she remembered, but when you only have twenty-six letters to work with, you don't have a lot of choices."

"Did you always leave messages on the board?"

She nodded. "I thought it was a game. She knew it was me, but she would pretend it was Hank or whatever. It gave her so much joy to tell me about the messages, I never stopped. I would always make sure she was upstairs or out of the house when I left one. I knew her life was pretty quiet, and it seemed like harmless fun."

"What about all the other ghostly signs? Like the lights flickering on and off?"

Lynne rolled her eyes. "There have always been lights blinking on and off in that house. For as long as I've known her, at least. When Hank was alive, he even said a few times he really needed to get the wiring looked at. Who knows how bad it is now."

"What about smelling Hank's scent?"

She made a face. "Yeah, I've smelled it too, from time to time. But you have to remember, she still has Hank's aftershave sitting in her bathroom cabinet. Not only that, but she still buys it. I always figured she might spray it around herself from time to time, just to feel closer to him."

"What about the toilet paper unrolling itself?"

"That's Sally. I've seen her do it myself. Sometimes I even replace the toilet roll for Ruth when Sally gets too … rambunctious." She shook her head. "I don't know why Ruth keeps replacing it the wrong way. I'm always trying to fix it for her, so the cat won't be able to make a mess of the bathroom."

"Did you do it before you left to see your daughter?"

Lynne frowned. "I think so. I can't really remember, but that seems right." She leaned closer to me. "Between you and me, that cat is something of a menace. If Ruth tells you about anything else getting moved or knocked over in the house, I have no doubt it's Sally."

The more I listened to Lynne, the stupider I felt. Of course there was a perfectly normal explanation for all of this. So why didn't we look for the reasonable explanation instead of literally chasing a ghost?

But I already knew why. Because that would mean one of us would have to explain to Ruth that there was no ghost, there never had been a ghost, and by the way … she needed to prepare herself to lose her home.

Ugh. I almost wished Scout *had* smelled a ghost. But obviously, what he had scented was Lynne, and she must have been the one to slam the back door.

"Did you also use the back door?"

Lynne looked troubled. "I did. I usually do, it feels less intrusive than going in and out of the front door. Plus, there's a key hidden in the backyard in case I ever forget mine. But something you said earlier … Ruth thought Hank left because she heard the back door slam shut? And then she saw the words on the message board?"

I nodded.

"Oh geez." Lynne rubbed her forehead, her expression grim. "That wasn't me."

"What do you mean? I thought you said you were the one who left 'bye' on the message board."

"I did. That was me. But she wasn't home when I left it. I had to get going fast—my daughter was in labor, and I wanted to be there for the birth, so I rushed over to Ruth's house to do a quick check to make sure everything was fine, and that's when I left the refrigerator magnet note."

"Wait a minute. You weren't there when Ruth came home from the grocery store?"

Lynne shook her head, her eyes wide. I could see the same horror in her eyes that was no doubt in mine.

Someone had been in Ruth's house.

Someone who had slammed the door.

"There's something else," Lynne said. "I was just packing up the car when I noticed someone hanging around Ruth's house."

My mouth dropped. "You saw someone? Bradley?"

She shook her head. "No, no, it wasn't Bradley. It was a woman."

A woman. I suddenly remembered Ruth describing seeing a woman, as well, after hearing the door slam. "What did she look like?"

"I couldn't see much. She had long, brown hair, I remember that. And she was a little on the heavy side. I got the impression she was in her forties or so, but I couldn't tell you why I thought that. She was kind of pacing around near Ruth's backyard, but when she saw me looking at her, she quickly turned and went the other direction. I almost went after her, but she disappeared so quickly, and I was already running late. I knew I needed to get on the road." She paused, biting her lower lip. "I should have gone after her. But honestly, I didn't get the sense that she wanted to hurt Ruth. For all I knew, she was one of those Jehovah's Witnesses. They come around every now and then. But … I should have made sure."

"It's not your fault," I said. "Even if she had been in Ruth's house …" a shiver ran down my spine just saying that, "she didn't hurt Ruth. I don't even think she took anything."

"So then why would she be there?" Lynne shook her head again. "Something isn't adding up."

I agreed. Something wasn't adding up. But that was because I was thinking about another older woman, with long, brown hair, who was a bit skittish. A woman who actually had a connection to Ruth … or, more specifically, to Ruth's husband.

Carly.

Chapter 19

It was nearly five o'clock by the time I pulled into The Dawn of Hope's parking lot. Carly was already outside, her back to me as she locked the door, her long, brown hair pulled back in a messy ponytail. I took a moment to quickly unroll the windows (so Scout wouldn't get too hot, although the day was already cooling off), and hurried over to her.

By the time I reached her, Carly had finished up and started to turn around. When she saw me, her eyes immediately narrowed, and her mouth started to open, probably to tell me she wasn't interested in talking to me, but I jumped in before she could form the words.

"I know who you are," I said.

She hesitated, and I saw a look of horror flash in her eyes, but it disappeared before I could be sure. "Of course you do. We met a couple of days ago. I'm Carly."

"You're Jazzy," I said.

She froze. Her mouth opened and closed a couple of times, but nothing came out. I thought she was trying to figure out whether she should deny it or not. Finally, she turned back to the door and started to unlock it. "You'd better come inside."

I didn't move. "Do you mind if I get my dog? He's friendly, and I would rather not leave him in the car."

She paused, and I could see her face softening. "Of course, I love dogs."

I hurried back to the car to fetch Scout while she went inside, and by the time Scout and I joined her, she was back in her office, sitting behind her desk, hands clasped in front of her.

"How did you know?" Her voice was soft, and she didn't look at me.

Scout ambled up to her, tail wagging, and started nosing her. Still without looking at me, she leaned over and started petting him, putting all her focus on him.

"I just put two and two together," I said before adding, "and you were seen by Ruth's neighbor."

She stopped petting Scout, and instead, her hands tightened on his fur. "I was repaying a debt." Her voice was so soft, I could barely hear her. "A debt I should have repaid a long time ago."

"Maybe you'd better start from the beginning," I said.

Carly didn't say anything for a moment, keeping her head down and taking long, deep breaths. "If I tell you the truth, can I trust you to keep it to yourself?"

"I'm not here to hurt you," I said. "I'm here for Ruth. She deserves the truth of what happened to her husband that day. I have no interest in outing you, but I would like to be able to share the truth with Ruth."

"Ruth does deserve the truth," she said quietly. "But what if the truth gets her killed?"

I felt like I had been dashed with ice-cold water. Goosebumps rose along my arms. "Why would the truth get her killed? Isn't Drake dead?"

"Yes, Drake is dead. Which is one of the reasons why I came back. But that doesn't mean it's safe. He still has followers." She raised her head to look me in the eye. "They still have girls."

"You came back to help them." It wasn't exactly a question, but she nodded.

"No one should have to go through what I did. But as important as getting the girls out is, I also had a debt to repay to Ruth."

"What was the debt?" I had started to brace myself, sure she was going to tell me that she had killed Hank.

"About twenty-thousand dollars."

I almost fell out of my chair. "What? How much?"

She almost smiled then. "I think you were right—I'd better start at the beginning. I met Hank because both of us had ... employers who were not exactly on the right side of the law. Hank never told me how he got sucked into helping cook the books for a seedy bar, along with a car wash and a laundromat that were most definitely fronts for money laundering. He said he had made some very big mistakes when he was younger, and he was being forced to pay for them. But because of those mistakes, he was bound and determined to ensure his wife never had to worry about money. He talked about how he was creating a nest egg for her, so that even if something were to happen to him, she would be taken care of."

"So, he wasn't your … client?" At the last moment, I couldn't say the word "john."

She burst out laughing. "Oh no. Hank never touched me." Her cheeks flushed. "Although I'm ashamed to say I tried. A couple of times. But no. He was absolutely not interested, although he was very kind when he turned me down. He said I was too sweet, and I reminded him of the daughter he never had." She turned pensive. "He loved Ruth very much."

We were both quiet for a moment, her thinking of Hank and me picturing Ruth, still so in love with her husband that she had convinced herself his ghost had come back to live with her.

Carly gave herself a quick shake. "Hank did his best to get me away from Drake. Along with Jean, of course. You have to understand, I was terrified. Not only of Drake, but also of the unknown. Where would I go if I left Drake? I couldn't go back home. My mother was a drug addict with a constant stream of druggy boyfriends who would do … well, suffice it to say, becoming a prostitute wasn't much of a stretch for me. I was at least getting paid.

"Hank did as much as he could. He would often buy me food, mostly dinner, but there was an occasional lunch as well. And yes, he had bought me lunch a few days before it … happened." Her fingers tightened again. "I found out later what the papers were reporting. It was too late to do much about it. I'm still angry that poor Ruth had to go through that."

She paused again, swallowing hard. "But if you want to know what happened that day … that terrible day … ironically, it was supposed to be a happy day. Hank had decided it was time to tell his wife the truth—or at least some version of the truth. I know he wasn't going to give her all the sordid details of where he made all that money over the years … but he had decided it was time. After he finished up that night, he had planned to take her out to a nice restaurant and tell her. I think …" she bit her lip. "No, I know, it was partly my fault. Those women from the office who saw us having lunch … I know it bothered him. He was worried someone was going to tell Ruth that he was seeing a prostitute. I never should have come to him that day, but I was starting to get really scared. I had this john who was getting weird. Almost obsessive. He had been following me and watching me and asking me questions about my other clients. It was creeping me out."

"But isn't Drake supposed to protect you from johns like that?" I asked.

Carly made a face. "That is the idea of a pimp, yes. But Drake only asked whether he hurt me or not. The answer was no, he hadn't hurt me. At least not physically. So Drake told me to quit worrying about it and take his money, and to let him know if he got violent or not. Of course, at that point, it might be too late for me, but Drake didn't really see things like that. To him, I wasn't much better than an animal, and only good if I was making him money. If I got hurt, well, it only meant that I couldn't bring any money in for him.

"But this guy … he was really scaring me. I was desperate, which is why I went to Hank to ask him what to do. He tried to get me to leave, but I was scared. Where would I go? What would happen if Drake tracked me down? But Hank was persistent, and I finally agreed to think about it. He said he would help me, and I believed him.

"The day he was going to come clean and tell his wife …" She stopped and licked her lips. Her hands had started to shake, and a few beads of sweat were dotting her forehead, even though the office was quite cool. "Steve approached me …"

"Steve?" The goosebumps were back, even though I told myself it must be a coincidence. Steve was a common name. But I wasn't sure I believed it.

"The name of the john. Or at least the name he told me to call him. I don't know whether it was his actual name or not. Anyway, he approached me and wanted his 'usual.' Normally, he would take me to a hotel or to his car, but this time, he was too impatient, and he had me follow him to that alley. I knew …" she stopped, licked her lips again. "I knew something was wrong. His eyes were glittering with a strange light. I thought maybe he was on something, like drugs or alcohol, because he normally wasn't like that.

"As soon as we got into the alley, he started yelling at me. Told me that I needed to stop sleeping with other men. I was his, and it was time I start acting like it.

"I tried to talk sense into him, but he was too far gone. Just kept telling me over and over that I was his, and if he couldn't have me, no one could. I was so terrified—I was sure that was it ... that he was going to kill me. But then, Hank was there."

"Hank?"

She nodded. "I know. He must have heard Steve yelling or ... I don't know. But there he was. He got between us and was trying to talk to Steve, to calm him down, when Steve just went berserk. Said the only reason why Hank was there was because Hank wanted me for himself, but he couldn't have me. Hank was trying to talk rationally to him, but Steve wouldn't listen. And then ... and then ..." Carly was shaking, and tears were streaming down her face. "Steve stabbed Hank."

I reached out to touch Carly's arm. She was still shaking, and the tears were flowing, so with my other hand, I grabbed a box of tissues and pushed it in front of her. She grabbed a handful and scrubbed at her face.

"Sorry," she said into a wet wad of tissues.

"You have nothing to be sorry about. I'm so sorry you had to witness that."

She nodded, still with the tissues pressed against her face, before finally straightening up. "After he stabbed Hank, Steve flipped out. He dropped the knife and ran. I was on my knees, trying to get the blood to stop, crying, begging for help, when I felt Hank press a large, manilla envelope into my hand. I didn't understand what he was doing and tried to push it away, tried to tell him to hang on, but he said, 'No, you take this. You get as far away as you can from here, and start a new life.' It finally dawned on me he was giving me his nest egg. Ruth's nest egg. I told him I couldn't take it, that it was Ruth's, but he shook his head. 'Ruth will be fine. She has my pension, and we have savings. She would want you to have it.'

"I was going to argue with him some more, but then Drake found us. He was furious. Of course he knew who Hank was—everyone did—he was the miracle accountant. Anyhow, he tore into me for killing Hank, but again, Hank intervened and said no, it wasn't me. It was one of my johns. And then I told Drake it was the crazy one, the one I had warned him about, but never mind that, we needed to get Hank help. But … it was too late. By the time Drake figured it out, Hank was …" She stopped again and scrubbed at her face.

"Drake was in a panic by then. He told me to go clean myself up, and he would take care of Hank. And Steve. I still had the envelope, and Drake hadn't yet realized I was carrying anything. The last thing I saw before I left the alley was Drake pulling Hank's pants down."

"Wait," I said, holding up a hand. "Drake was the one who pulled down Hank's pants?"

"That back alley was known for prostitution. I think Drake thought it might be easier if everyone assumed Hank had brought it on himself."

"So what did you do?"

She looked at me, her eyes wet. "I did what Hank asked me to do with his dying breath. I ran."

We were both silent. She was lost in the nightmare of that one awful moment that changed everything, not just for her but for Ruth as well, and probably others. Me wondering just how far down the rabbit hole this all went.

Scout pressed his nose into Carly's hand, and she sucked in a shaky breath as she started to pet him again. "I'm not proud of it. A part of me wishes I hadn't … that I had stayed and told the police what happened. That I had given Ruth her money. That I didn't let them lie and smear Hank's good name and reputation." She paused again, staring off into the distance. "But I was so scared. It's not an excuse, I know that. But it's the only one I have."

"You shouldn't blame yourself," I said. "None of this is your fault."

"It's my fault for running."

"You were a kid," I said. "You were in a dreadful situation. Let's say you had stayed and told the cops and tried to turn over the money to Ruth. There's no guarantee the cops would have believed you. You could have gone to jail for Hank's death. Or you could have ended up back in Drake's clutches. And there's certainly no guarantee Ruth would have ever gotten that money."

"I know the arguments," Carly said quietly. "Believe me, I've repeated them to other girls in my situation enough times. But it doesn't change the guilt. Maybe I should have gone to jail. Maybe Drake should have killed me. I don't know." She held up a hand. "Look, I didn't tell you all of this because I wanted to argue about it. Just so you would understand why I came back."

I closed my mouth and gave her a little nod to continue. It was easy for me to tell her that none of this was her fault. Watching Hank die because he stepped in to save her, then give her the money meant for his wife, must have been difficult for her, even as desperate as she was.

"I left Redemption. That night. I almost didn't even go back to my room, but I was covered in blood. I knew that would raise too many questions. I changed my clothes, cleaned up as much as I dared, threw a few things into a duffle bag along with the money, and ran. Within the hour, I was buying a ticket at the bus station for the next bus out of town. I spent the first year on the run, barely staying anywhere for longer than a day or so. I knew Drake had spies everywhere; it was uncanny how fast he found girls. If I hadn't had Hank's money ..." She gave her head a quick shake. "Anyway, eventually, I stopped running. I had reinvented myself as Carly, with a brand-new ID, courtesy of an underground network that helped abused wives disappear. I never told them I hadn't married my abuser, but they didn't seem to care that much. I got a job as a waitress and went to nursing school. I knew I needed a job where I could make enough to live on while I paid back Hank. It took longer than I wanted, but I did it. I took every overtime opportunity I could. I worked nights, weekends, holidays, while spending the bare minimum I needed to live. It wasn't easy, but I did it. I saved the money.

"The next part was trickier. How do I get the money to Ruth without drawing attention to myself or to her? I was too afraid to chance it while Drake was still alive. Once I knew he was dead, I thought it was possible. I could come back for a day. Show up, give the money to Ruth, and leave. Easy peasy.

"But then I heard that The Dawn of Hope was looking for a new director. Since Jean retired and moved to Florida, they hadn't been able to find anyone who was willing to do it. I wasn't going to do it. I already had a life. A job. Why would I possibly want to move back to a town full of violence and death? A town I still had nightmares about?

"But then I remembered how hard they had worked to save me. How it was because of what they told me that I had been able to save myself. They were the ones who told me about the underground networks that helped abused women. They had taught me ways of hiding and running. So, I applied for the job. And the board hired me on the spot."

She smiled slightly at the memory. "Trust me, it wasn't because I was such a great applicant. I'm pretty sure they were desperate at the time. But it didn't matter. I knew I was where I was supposed to be. In the mouth of madness, so to speak. It made no sense, but I knew it in my gut. Money didn't matter. I had saved enough, more than enough, to pay Ruth back. I just had to give it to her. Which ended up turning into the second problem."

She glanced at me, her smile turning bitter. "I couldn't do it. Every day, I would think to myself 'Today is the day I'll go to Ruth's house and give her the money.' I could picture it in my head. Knocking on the door, explaining who I was, telling her how I owed Hank my life, handing her the envelope. The money was there. I had already taken it out of the bank and had put it in a big brown envelope—the same one Hank had it in originally. And every day, I would somehow never make it to Ruth's house. I was too busy; I had to work late; I had to run errands; I had a board meeting; I had this, I had that." Her face was filled with disgust at herself. "It was shameful, really. I should be ashamed of myself. I was ashamed of myself. But no matter how much I told myself how terrible I was acting, I couldn't bring myself to do it. I couldn't bear the thought of standing in front of Hank's widow, the woman who had taken on so much pain because of me, and confessing to her that I had had the power to have stopped it, and didn't.

"Finally I'd had enough. I was sick of myself. I could tell myself all I wanted that I was only interested in keeping Ruth safe, and while that was true to a point, it wasn't the whole story. I needed to stop making excuses and do the right thing, and I needed to do it now.

"So I went to Ruth's house. I parked a couple of blocks away, as I didn't want to draw any attention to either her or me, and walked to her house. I marched up to her front door and rang the doorbell.

"And no one answered."

She gave me a bemused look. "At that point, I didn't know what to do. I was a little afraid that if I left, I might never come back, so I started to walk around the property, thinking maybe if there was an open door, I could just leave the envelope inside and be done with it. That was when the neighbor saw me. I quickly ran off and hid, and it was while I was watching her finish loading up the car and driving off that I realized I needed to pay this debt and move on. For both of us.

"Once the neighbor left, I started trying the doors again, but of course, they were all locked. I started looking for a key, and I found one. In the backyard, by the back door, so I tried it on that door. It took a bit, but I got the door open and had just stepped inside when I heard the voice. It was Ruth. And it sounded like she was talking to someone. Actually, it sounded like she was angry with someone, like they were having a fight. Did that mean someone was in the house after all? I panicked and shoved the envelope on the counter next to the back door and left as fast as I could, but in my haste, I accidentally slammed the door shut. I was so panicked, I practically ran from the house, only slowing down when I got about a block away."

She paused, dropping her face into her hands. "It's even worse saying it out loud. I truly am a coward."

"You're not a coward," I said automatically as my mind was spinning. Again, I saw Scout pawing at the counter next to the backdoor, digging at it, like … there was something there. "Did you say you put the envelope with the money in it on that counter right next to the back door?"

Chapter 20

As it turned out, the envelope of money had fallen in the crack between the counter and the door. Scout had found it after all. And it was more than enough to not only pay all the back taxes, but get the rest of Ruth's finances in order, too.

Getting Ruth to report Bradley/Steven was another matter. After a lot of talking, Aunt Tilde and Mildred were finally able to convince her. Also, I suspected learning the real reason why Bradley/Steven had targeted her had a little something to do with it, as well.

Carly's crazy stalker, the man who also killed Hank, was Steven's father. Once Drake realized it wasn't going to be that easy to find Carly, Drake had turned his attention and frustration to Steve, eventually tracking him down and killing him.

It wasn't clear how Steven was able to piece it all together. My guess is his father gave him enough details before he was killed that Steven figured it out. He had wanted to kill Drake, but someone else got to Drake before he could, so he took his revenge out on Hank's widow, the man who, in his mind, was the cause of his father's death. Steven was currently sitting in jail for stealing from Ruth. Whether or not she would be able to get her money back was still up for debate, but at least her house was safe.

I had been dreading telling Ruth about not being able to find Hank's ghost, but as it turned out, it didn't matter. Ruth decided the reason why Hank had left that day was because Carly had returned Hank's money, so Hank no longer needed to protect Ruth. Oddly enough, the wiring issues also seemed to have cleared up, as both Aunt Tilde and Lynne reported no more blinking lights. Nor were there any more aftershave scents.

I was sure it was just a coincidence. At least, pretty sure.

Ruth also, at Aunt Tilde and Mildred's suggestion, had decided to get more involved with the living. She joined the local adult community center and started showing up at the local game nights to play Bingo and Sheepshead, which is a complicated Wisconsin card game that I never really got the hang of.

Ruth also thought she might want to join The Redemption Detective Agency. Aunt Tilde thought that was a great idea. I wasn't nearly as excited. I was secretly hoping Ruth was busy enough with all her game nights, as the last thing I needed was yet another "detective" to keep track of. Although it wouldn't matter what Ruth did if I left.

Jerome was pressuring me to fill out the job application he'd given me, which I had every intention of doing. As he kept pointing out, it made no sense to stay where I was. It would be better for my career if I took the school secretary job. I knew he was right.

But before I left, I had to wrap up a few things, which was how I found myself standing in front of Stewart and Associates one morning.

When I told Aunt Tilde my plan, I had almost told her I was doing it for her, as well. So she no longer had to volunteer her time to help Nick out. After everything Aunt Tilde had done for me, I thought it was the least I could do. But she hadn't told me about her real estate business, and at the last minute, I decided not to say anything. If she wanted me to know, she would tell me.

As for me, I had debts of my own to pay back. Not just for Aunt Tilde, but for Nick.

My palms were sweaty, and I wiped them off on my jeans before reaching for the door. The morning was cool, but I could still feel beads of sweat trickle down the back of my dark-blue silk blouse. Ugh. I hadn't worn a jacket for this exact reason. But it was too late to do anything about it, so hopefully, Nick wouldn't notice.

I opened the door and stepped into the waiting room. I could see Nick sitting at his desk, surrounded by towering stacks of paper. The sleeves of his white shirt were rolled up, and his navy tie was crooked. He glanced up, and a lock of hair fell over his forehead. My gut clenched, and I was having trouble breathing.

"Emily. What a surprise." He stood up to walk around the desk, a mask of professionalism on his face, but I caught a glimpse of something close to concern before the mask snapped back into place. "Is everything okay?" He craned his neck to look behind me.

I rubbed my hands against my jeans again as I tried telling myself I was being silly. There was no reason to be nervous. "Everything is fine."

His face relaxed, and his lips quirked up in a wolfish grin. "Oh, well then how can I help you?"

Ugh. Maybe this was a bad idea after all. Maybe I should rethink this and figure out another way to pay him back. But even as I was debating, I saw one of the stacks of paper start to tip over and fall to the floor, and I knew I had no choice but to stay. "Actually, I'm here to help you."

His eyebrows bunched together. "Help me?"

I nodded. "I'm going to organize your office for you." As soon as the words were out of my mouth, my chest started to loosen up. Yes, this was exactly what I needed to be doing. The sooner I got his office organized, the better we would all feel.

He gave me a surprised look. "You are? Why?"

"Because you need the help, and it's what I'm good at."

He studied me, a knowing expression on his face. "And Aunt Tilde isn't?"

"Well, we all have our talents," I said.

At that, he did smile, and once again, I felt my breath catch. "Well, who am I to turn away an expert office manager? Please, have at it." He swung his arm out in a flourish as he stepped away from the door. "Can I work in my office while you work your magic?"

"Of course. It's your office," I said, even though I wasn't sure if I would be able to do a thing if he was in there with me. No, this was crazy. I needed to pull myself together. We were both professionals.

His grin widened. "Well, I must say this will make coming to work that much more interesting. Does this mean you've decided to stay at The Redemption Detective Agency?"

I froze. My mouth seemed to dry up, and I wasn't sure if I was going to be able to speak. I forced myself to swallow and felt like I was choking. What was wrong with me? Maybe this really was a bad idea, and I should just leave. Immediately.

Nick gave me a curious look, and I forced myself to relax and take a deep breath. "Actually, I decided to take the job."

It was as if a curtain fell across Nick's face. "I see." His voice was cool, and his eyes had shuttered.

I took another deep breath as I stumbled on. "I haven't told Aunt Tilde yet, so if you could … keep it to yourself. I want to finish a few things up before I go, so …"

"You don't have to explain. I get it." He had already turned away from me. I could almost feel the chill, and the sweat that had been dripping down my back suddenly turned to ice. "Let me know if you need anything from me. I have a couple of appointments this morning, so I'll be back in a few hours. Will that be fine for you?"

"Sure," I said faintly, watching as Nick strode to the door and opened it without a backward glance. My stomach had twisted into all sorts of knots, and I had a terrible feeling that I had just made a huge mistake. A part of me wanted to call out after him to say … what? What would I tell him? He had a girlfriend, and I had a boyfriend. What was there to talk about? It wasn't even like I was leaving Redemption, just the detective agency.

It took me another few moments, but eventually, I turned around and headed into Nick's office. I should be glad he was out. It would make everything a lot easier if he weren't there. I should be grateful.

But no matter how much I kept telling myself that, I couldn't make myself believe it.

A Word From Michele

Want more Emily, Nick and the gang? Keep going with Book 4, *The Mysterious Case of the Missing House*.

Preorder your copy right here.

MPWNovels.com/book/the-mysterious-case-of-the-missing-house

The Redemption Detective Agency is a spin-off from *The Charlie Kingsley Mysteries*. If you want to see where it all began, take a look at *The Murder Before Christmas*.

https://MPWNovels.com/r/bghostchristmaswide

****

You can also check out exclusive bonus content for *The Redemption Detective Agency* here, including a scene told from Nick's point of view when he meets Emily. https://mpwnovels.com/mpw-book-club/

The bonus content reveals hints, clues, and sneak peeks you won't get just by reading the books, so you'll definitely want to check it out. You're going to discover a side of Redemption that is only available here.

***

If you enjoyed *The Mysterious Case of the Missing Ghost*, it would be wonderful if you would take a few minutes to leave a review and rating on Amazon:

amazon.com/dp/B0DJ7WTMS2/

Goodreads:

goodreads.com/book/show/219755152-the-mysterious-case-of-the-missing-ghost

or Bookbub:

bookbub.com/books/the-mysterious-case-of-the-missing-ghost-the-redemption-detective-agency-book-3-by-michele-pw-pariza-wacek

(Feel free to follow me on any of those platforms as well.) I thank you and other readers will thank you (as your reviews will help other readers find my books.)

All my series are interconnected and related, and if you'd like to learn more about them, take a look at my website MPWNovels.com. You'll also discover lots of other fun things such as short stories, deleted scenes, giveaways, recipes, puzzles and more.

I've also included a sneak peek of *The Murder Before Christmas* if you'd like to check it out. Just turn the page to get started.

The Murder Before Christmas
Chapter 1

"So, Courtney, is it?" I asked with what I hoped was a comforting and nonthreatening smile. I set the mug holding my newest tea blend I'd created for the Christmas season—a variety of fresh mint and a couple of other secret ingredients—down on the kitchen table. I called it "Candy Cane Concoctions", and hoped others would find it as soothing as it was refreshing. "What can I do for you?"

Courtney didn't look at me as she reached for her tea. She was young, younger than me, and extremely pretty, despite looking like something the cat dragged in. (And believe me, I know all about what cats can drag in. Midnight, my black cat, had presented me with more than my share of gifts over the years.) Courtney's long, wavy blonde hair was pulled back in a haphazard ponytail, and there were puffy, black circles under her china-blue eyes. She was also visibly pregnant.

"Well, Mrs. Kingsley," she began, but I quickly interrupted her.

"It's Miss, but please, call me Charlie." Yes, she was younger than me, but for goodness sake, not THAT much younger. Maybe it was time to start getting more serious about my morning makeup routine.

Her lips quirked up in a tiny smile that didn't quite reach her eyes. "Charlie, then. I was hoping you could make me a love potion."

I quickly dropped my gaze, busying myself by pushing the plate of frosted Christmas sugar cookies I had made earlier toward her, not wanting her to see my shock and sorrow. She was pregnant and wanted a love potion. This just couldn't be good.

"I don't actually do love potions," I said. "I make custom-blended teas and tinctures."

Her eyebrows knit together in confusion. "But people have been raving about how much you've helped them. Mrs. Witmore swears you cured her thyroid problems."

I tried not to sigh. "My teas and tinctures do have health benefits, that's true. Certain herbs and flowers can help with common ailments. In fact, for much of human civilization, there were no prescription drugs, so all they had to use were herbs and flowers. But I can't promise any cures."

"What about Ruthie?" Courtney asked. "She claims those heart tinctures you made are the reason Bob finally noticed her."

I gritted my teeth. When Ruthie's dad was recovering from a heart attack, I made a couple of teas and tinctures for him. Ruthie, who had a crush on her coworker Bob for years, was apparently so desperate for him to notice her that one day, she decided to bring one of my tinctures to work (I'm unclear which) and slip it into his drink. And apparently, shortly after that, Bob started up a conversation with her, and eventually asked her out on a date.

It didn't help matters that Jean, Ruthie's mother, had claimed my tinctures had reignited her and her husband's love life, which is probably how Ruthie got the idea to try them with Bob in the first place.

Needless to say, that was an unintended benefit.

"I didn't give Ruthie a love potion," I said. "I gave her dad some tinctures and teas to help his heart."

Courtney gazed at me with those clear-blue eyes, reminding me of a broken-down, worn-out doll. "Well, isn't that where love starts?"

"Maybe," I said. "But my intention was to heal her father's heart, not to make anyone fall in love with anyone else."

"But it worked," she said. "Can you just sell me whatever you gave her? I have money. I'll pay."

"It's not that simple," I said. "I really need to ask you some questions. It's always good to talk to your doctor, as well."

She bit her lip and dropped her gaze to the tea in her hands. She looked so lost and alone, I felt sorry for her.

"Why don't you tell me a little bit about who you want this love potion for?" I asked. "That would help me figure out how best to help you."

She didn't immediately answer, instead keeping her eyes down. Just as I was starting to think she wasn't going to say anything at all, she spoke. "It's for my husband," she said, her voice so low, it was nearly a whisper.

I could feel my heart sink to the floor. This was even more heartbreaking than I had imagined. "You think your husband fell out of love with you?"

"I know he has," she said. "He's having an affair."

"Oh Courtney," I sighed. "I'm so sorry to hear that."

She managed a tiny nod and picked up her tea to take a sip.

"Have you two talked about it?"

She shook her head quickly.

"Does he know you know?"

She shrugged.

"Maybe that's the place to start," I said, keeping my voice gentle. "Having a conversation."

"It won't help," she said, her voice still quiet.

"How do you know if you haven't tried?"

She didn't answer … just stared into her tea.

"Have you thought about marriage counseling?"

"He won't go." Her voice was firm.

"Have you asked?"

"I know. He's said before he thinks therapy is a waste of money."

"Okay. But you have a baby on the way," I said. "You need to be able to talk through things. I understand it might be difficult to talk about something like *this*, but ..."

"He's in love with her." The words burst out of her as she raised her head. The expression on her face was so anguished that for a moment, it took my breath away.

"But how do you know if you haven't talked to him about it?"

"I just do," she said. "When you're married, you know these things. You can sense when your husband has fallen out of love with you. Hence, my need for a love potion. I need him to fall back in love with me. You can see how urgent this is." She gestured to her stomach. "In a few months, we're going to have a baby. I just *have* to get him to fall back in love with me."

Oh man, this was not going well. "I see why you would think that would be easier, but the problem is, there's no such thing as a love potion."

"Can you please just sell me what you made for Ruthie's dad? So I can at least try?"

"Whatever happened between Ruthie and Bob had nothing to do with one of my tinctures," I said flatly. "I don't want to give you false hope. I really think your best course of action is to have an open and honest conversation with him about the affair."

She was noticeably disappointed. It seemed to radiate out of every pore. I hated being the one to cause that, but I also wasn't going to sell her anything that could be misconstrued as a "love potion." Not only for her sake, but my own. The last thing I needed was lovesick women showing up at my door to buy something that didn't exist.

"Okay," she said quietly as she ducked her head so I couldn't quite see her face. "No love potion. How about the opposite?"

I looked at her in confusion. "The opposite?"

"Yes. Something that would kill him."

My mouth fell open. "Wha ... I'm sorry, could you repeat that?" I must have heard her wrong. She was still talking so quietly, not to mention hiding her face.

Courtney blinked and looked up at me. "I'm sorry?"

"I didn't hear what you said. Could you repeat it?"

"Oh. It was nothing." She offered an apologetic smile.

"No, really," I said. "I thought ..." I laughed a little self-consciously. "I thought you said you wanted something to kill your husband."

She blinked again. "Oh. Yeah. It was just a joke."

"A joke?"

"Yeah. I mean, you know. Sometimes married people want to kill each other. No big deal." Now it was her turn to let out a little twitter of laughter. "Have you ever been married?"

I shivered and put my hands around my mug to absorb the warmth. "No." Which was true. I had never been officially married, but that didn't mean my love life wasn't ... complicated.

Nor did it mean I didn't know exactly what she was talking about.

"Well, you know, sometimes married people can just get really angry with each other, and in the heat of the moment, even want to kill each other," she explained. "But they don't mean it. It's just because they love each other so much that sometimes that passion looks like something else. In the heat of the moment, in the middle of a fight, you can say all sorts of things you don't mean. But of course, they wouldn't *do* anything about it."

"Of course," I said. I decided not to mention that when she said it, she wasn't actually arguing with her husband. Nor did I bring up how perhaps she was protesting a bit too much.

I gave her a hard look as I sipped my tea.

She kept her gaze firmly on the table, refusing to meet my eyes. "Did I tell you how wonderful this blend is?" she asked. "It's so refreshing. Reminds me of a candy cane."

"Thanks. It's called 'Candy Cane Concoctions,' actually. I created it for the holidays," I said.

"It's wonderful." She took another hurried drink and put her mug down, tea sloshing over the side. "Are you selling it? Could I buy some?"

"Sure," I said, getting up from my chair. "Hang on a minute. I'll get you a bag."

She nodded as I left the kitchen to head upstairs to my office/work room. Although, to be fair, it was so small, it wasn't uncommon to find drying herbs or plants throughout the house.

I collected a bag and headed back to the kitchen. When I walked in, Courtney was standing up, fiddling with her purse. I instantly felt like something was off. Maybe it was the way she was standing or the bend of her neck, but she oozed guilt.

"Oh, there you are," she said, fishing out her wallet. "How much do I owe you?'

I told her, and she pulled out a wad of cash, handing me a twenty.

"I'll have to get you some change," I said.

"That's not necessary," she said, taking the bag. "You were so helpful to me, and besides, I need to get going."

"But this is way too much," I protested. "Just let me find my purse."

She waved me off as she left the kitchen and headed for the front door. "Nonsense. Truly, you were very helpful. No change is necessary." She jammed her arms into her coat, and without bothering to zip it up, opened the front door and headed out into the cold.

I closed the door after her, watching her through the window as she made her way down the driveway and into her car. She didn't seem very steady on her feet, and I wanted to make sure she got into her vehicle safely. After she drove off, I went back to the kitchen to look around.

Nothing appeared to be out of order. If she had been digging around looking for something (like something to kill her husband with), it wasn't obvious.

Still, I couldn't shake that uneasy feeling.

I went to the table to collect the dishes. Midnight strolled in as I was giving myself a pep talk.

"I'm sure she didn't mean it," I said to him. "She was probably just upset. I mean, she wasn't getting her love potion, and clearly, she was uncomfortable having a conversation with her husband. Although you'd think that would be a red flag."

Midnight sat down, his dark-green eyes studying me.

"Of course, that's hardly my business," I continued. "She's upset with him, and rightfully so. Who wouldn't be? Even if she wasn't actually joking in the moment, she was surely just letting off steam."

Midnight's tail twitched.

"Maybe this was even the first time she said it out loud," I said as I moved to the sink. "And now that she said it, she realized how awful it was. Of course she would never do anything like that." I turned to the cat. "Right?"

Midnight started cleaning himself.

"You're a lot of help," I muttered, turning back to the sink to finish the washing up.

As strange as that encounter was, it was likely the end of it.

I hoped.

Want to keep reading? Grab your copy of *The Murder Before Christmas* here:

MPWNovels.com/r/bghostmbcamzn

Books and series by Michele Pariza Wacek

Redemption Detective Agency
(Cozy Mysteries)
A spin-off from the Charlie Kingsley series.
https://MPWNovels.com/r/da_ghost

Charlie Kingsley Mysteries
(Cozy Mysteries)
See all of Charlie's adventures here.
https://MPWnovels.com/r/ck_ghost

Secrets of Redemption series
(Pychological Thrillers)
The flagship series that started it all.
https://MPWnovels.com/r/rd_ghost

Mysteries of Redemption
(Psychological Thrillers)
A spin-off from the Secrets of Redemption series.
https://MPWnovels.com/r/mr_ghost

Riverview Mysteries
(standalone Pychological Thrillers)
*These stories take place in Riverview, which is near
Redemption.*
https://MPWnovels.com/r/rm_ghost

Access your free exclusive bonus scenes from *The Mysterious Case of
the Missing Ghost* right here:
MPWnovels.com/r/q/redemption-agency-bonus/

Acknowledgements

It's a team effort to birth a book, and I'd like to take a moment to thank everyone who helped, especially my wonderful editor, Megan Yakovich, who is always so patient with me, and my husband Paul, for his love and support during this sometimes-painful birthing process.

Any mistakes are mine and mine alone.

About Michele

A USA Today Bestselling, award-winning author, Michele taught herself to read at 3 years old because she wanted to write stories so badly. It took some time (and some detours) but she does spend much of her time writing stories now. Mystery stories, to be exact. They're clean and twisty, and range from psychological thrillers to cozies, with a dash of romance and supernatural thrown into the mix. If that wasn't enough, she posts lots of fun things on her blog, including short stories, puzzles, recipes and more, at MPWNovels.com.

Michele grew up in Wisconsin, (hence why all her books take place there), and still visits regularly, but she herself escaped the cold and now lives in the mountains of Prescott, Arizona with her husband and southern squirrel hunter Cassie.

When she's not writing, she's usually reading, hanging out with her dog, or watching the Food Network and imagining she's an awesome cook. (Spoiler alert, she's not. Luckily for the whole family, Mr. PW is in charge of the cooking.)

191